The Calling

Philip Caveney

Published by Fledgling Press 2016

Cover Design: Kylie Tesdale

Printed and bound by:
MBM Print SCS Ltd, Glasgow

ISBN: 9781905916085

MIX
Paper from
responsible sources
FSC® C117931
FSC
www.fsc.org

ONE

Arrival

The boy opened his eyes…

He had the distinct impression that he was surfacing from deep underwater, rising slowly to meet the rippling surface. At first, everything was blurred. He was aware only of sound and movement, his vision an uncertain fog of muddy colours. Then everything came sharply into focus.

He was on a train, he decided, which was odd, because he didn't remember getting *on* a train or even having the intention of doing so. He looked slowly around, blinking like somebody who had just emerged from a deep sleep. Perhaps he had.

It was packed, this train – heaving with people, some standing in the aisle, others seated and balancing heavy bags on their laps, perhaps because the proper luggage areas were too full. The boy realised that he was sitting at a table. Opposite him, an elderly couple, a man and a woman, were pulling on jackets as though preparing to leave. The boy stared at them helplessly. He didn't know who they were, he was pretty certain he'd never seen them before but he couldn't even be sure of that, because…

He didn't know who he was.

He didn't know what he was doing on this train or where he was going or why he had got on it in the first place. It dawned on him in a sudden rush of anxiety that he didn't even know his own name.

He turned his head to look at the person sitting next to him, hoping it might be somebody he recognised, but it was a middle-aged man in a black suit who was pushing a laptop into an expensive-looking leather case, a man with the cold uncaring face of a stranger.

The elderly woman must have caught his look of confusion, because she smiled at him and said, 'Are you all right, dear?'

He nodded, but didn't know why he'd done that, because actually he *wasn't* all right, he was scared and confused and he was trying to piece things together in his own mind, trying to remember what had brought him here, but it was like groping around in the mud at the bottom of a pond. There was only darkness in his recent past, a thick veil of sludge that he couldn't seem to see through or get any kind of grip on.

'Is somebody meeting you?' asked the woman, clearly trying to be helpful and he could only shrug and smile like an idiot, because he didn't *know* if anybody was meeting him, he didn't know *anything*. He thought about telling her that, but for some reason decided against it. He'd sound like an idiot, he decided. No, he needed to pull his thoughts together before he went speaking to people. He needed to get a grip.

As if to mirror his thoughts, the train slipped abruptly into shadow. He turned to look out of the window and saw that it was entering a grey stone tunnel. For an instant his reflection stared back at him from the glass. He saw a boy of about twelve or thirteen years old, he thought, a boy with dark hair and a face he didn't recognise. Then a voice came over the tannoy, a man's voice speaking with what sounded like a Scottish accent.

'We will shortly be arriving at Edinburgh Waverley where this train terminates. Will passengers please ensure they have all of their personal belongings before leaving the train?'

The voice seemed to act as a kind of goad. Suddenly everyone was up on their feet, pulling on coats, heaving down bags from the luggage racks overhead. The boy looked up at the glass shelf immediately above him, wondering if one the bags stored there might be his, but as he watched, eager hands removed item after item, until there was nothing left.

And then the train emerged from darkness and slid slowly into the station and he saw a sign announcing that this was indeed, *Edinburgh Waverley*. The boy knew that Edinburgh was in Scotland, but as far as he was aware, he had never been here before and had no reason to be here now, because he lived in…

No.

Nothing. Another blank. This was beginning to feel really scary. His heart seemed to leap in his chest.

The train lurched to a stop, the doors pinged open and the exodus began, everybody seemingly intent on getting off the train as quickly as possible. The boy hung back, not wanting to be caught up in the frantic press of bodies. The elderly woman gave him one last concerned look, as though she might be thinking of asking him more questions, but her husband was clearly anxious to be on the move, one hand clutching her arm, his expression saying 'don't get involved,' so after a moment's hesitation, she followed him out into the aisle and off towards the doors. The boy sat there, staring out of the window at the heaving platform, thinking that he really ought to try and come up with some kind of plan, but nothing useful occurred to him and after a little while, there was just him sitting alone in the empty carriage. Then a uniformed man came along the aisle with a bin bag, picking up rubbish from the tables as he came. He paused and gave the boy an odd look.

'You not getting off?' he asked indignantly.

'Er… yeah, sure.' The boy got obediently to his feet and shuffled sideways into the aisle. He turned and headed for the nearest door. He came to a luggage rack and paused to see if anybody had left a bag or a case behind, but it was empty. He frowned then, aware that the uniformed man was still looking at him, went out through the exit doors and onto the platform.

It was incredibly busy out there, people sweeping to and fro, like a colony of ants all engaged in important business, most people dragging huge suitcases on wheels behind them. The boy joined the tail end of a long procession heading towards some exit gates and noticed, as the queue began to shorten, that people were displaying tickets to a man standing at some electronic barriers. He was using a plastic card to open and shut them, allowing only one or two people through at a time.

The boy knew enough to realise that he ought to have some kind of ticket for travel, so he started rooting in the pockets of his jeans. He pulled out a handful of coins from one pocket, a piece of folded paper from the other and a single metal key. The queue in front of him was rapidly shortening and the man at the gate didn't look the sympathetic sort, so the boy tried the pockets of the jacket he was wearing, a hooded khaki affair. He found various bits of detritus but nothing that resembled a railway ticket and now he saw that he was next in line and he began to panic. The man ahead of him went through the barrier and it snapped shut behind him. The guard turned his baleful gaze to the boy. He was a thickset man with cold blue eyes and a stubbled chin.

'Ticket?' he snapped.

The boy looked at him helplessly. 'I don't… I can't… it's…'

'TICKET!' growled the guard, looking irritably at the long queue forming behind the boy.

'I haven't… I can't find…' The boy couldn't see any other way out of this. 'I don't know who I am!' he said.

A strange expression came over the guard's grumpy face. He looked weary, as though this was something that happened to him all the time. He rolled his eyes, shook his head, then waved his card in front of the barrier, making it slide magically open. 'Go on,' he said. 'Get moving.'

'But…'

'NEXT!' roared the guard and the boy jumped forward, galvanised by the urgency in the man's voice. Then he was following other travellers across a flat stretch of tarmac and up a steep ramp to the open air.

TWO

Edinburgh

He emerged into even greater chaos. It was late afternoon, judging by the long shadows, and the street was crowded with people, all of them pushing and shoving their way towards a line of black cabs parked alongside the kerb, so he detached himself from that queue and headed to his right, following the pavement across a wide bridge that was thronged with busy traffic. He had to push and shove his way through the other people heading in both directions on the crowded pavement. When he got to the far side of the bridge, a weird sound assailed his ears, something that sounded like the caterwauling of a tortured animal. Looking around, he saw a band of musicians on the far side of the road. They were playing some kind of rocked-up Scottish folk tune: a guitarist, a drummer and a man playing bagpipes, who was leaping up and down on the spot like somebody demented. The band was standing beside the open gates of a park and an eager crowd were gathered in front of them, clapping their hands and urging them on.

The park's entrance seemed to offer some respite from the bustle and noise, so when he got to the top of the road, he waited for the lights to change and crossed over, noticing as he did so how every lamppost along the street was decorated with a colourful poster, advertising a whole series of events, most of them featuring a grinning face. He thought he recognised one or two of the faces, decided he'd seen them before, possibly on TV, but he couldn't be sure. A name accompanied each face and though some of the names had a familiar ring to them, he couldn't have said with any certainty who any of these people actually were.

He made it to the far side of the road and paused for a moment to stare at the band. Close up, they sounded quite fearsome, the drummer bashing at his miniature kit with manic energy, the sound of his bass drum seeming to thud like a series of punches to the boy's chest. As he watched, a couple of people broke from the crowd and moved forward to throw coins into a hat on the pavement, but the boy didn't feel he could spare any of the money he'd found in his pocket, so instead he went in through the gates and descended a long flight of stone steps to a wide path some ten feet below the level of the street.

It was a bit quieter here, though still busy with people. The sounds of the traffic receded as the boy walked along. On the horizon, away to his left, perched on a high clump of rock stood what could only be described as a castle. It looked like something from a fairy tale, the boy thought, but he managed to make some kind of a connection with the word Edinburgh. There *was* an Edinburgh Castle, wasn't there? He wasn't sure how he knew this, but it felt right and for the first time since he'd opened his eyes he felt a little cheered. At least there was *something* he thought he knew. He kept walking. He went past long rows of park benches and a little café serving coffee and ice cream. People sitting at outdoor tables were enjoying the last rays of the afternoon sunshine, but the peaceful scene was short-lived because, all too soon, he reached the far end of the park and had nowhere else to go but back up onto the busy road. As he came out of the gates he caught sight of a road sign announcing that he was on Princes Street. Buses and trams rumbled past him and a seemingly never-ending stream of black cabs.

Thinking that it might be quieter on the far side of the road, he crossed over and found himself heading down narrower streets, but the crowds were no thinner here, so he headed up a steep hill that curved slowly around to his left. The railings that flanked the pavement along the route were now an endless procession of garish posters, advertising comedy nights, theatre events, musicals, concerts… Edinburgh clearly was a very busy place.

He reached the top of the hill, a crossroads, and paused for a moment, wondering which way to go. To his right there was a big black and white pub where throngs of people stood outside drinking beer and wine. A prominent sign announced that this was '*Deacon Brodie's Tavern.*' The boy turned left away from it and started walking down the cobbled street beyond, but he'd only gone a short distance when he realised that he'd made a mistake. The way ahead was absolutely choked with people, many of whom seemed to be in fancy dress, some of them carrying placards for various shows, and as he walked along some of them started approaching him, offering him sheets of paper advertising the different events.

'Do you like comedy?' asked a man who was dressed as some kind of Space Pirate, pushing a leaflet into his hands. '*Captain Danger and the Super Vixens from Venus,*' he added mysteriously. 'Starts in ten minutes, just up the street there.'

The boy didn't know what to say. He took the leaflet and started to walk on, only to be accosted by a young woman dressed as some kind of medieval wench. '*The Crucible!*' she barked in his face, displaying rows of teeth that had been artificially blackened – at least, the boy *hoped* that was the case. 'Arthur Miller's brilliant play about the Salem Witch trials, Pleasance Courtyard, seven o'clock tonight. Special discount with this flyer.'

'Er... thanks,' said the boy, taking the sheet from her, though he really didn't have much idea what she was on about. As if at some signal, others in the crowd appeared to sense that he was an easy target. There was a sudden rush and he found himself wading though a sea of humanity, every one of whom was intent on shoving a sheet of brightly-coloured paper at him. He'd accepted a dozen of them before he began to gaze frantically around, looking for some avenue of escape. He saw an opportunity and ducked behind a large metal litterbin, then ran around it, only to find himself standing beside a makeshift wooden stage, where a group of what he thought might be Spanish dancers in colourful costumes were whirling and spinning to amplified guitar music. One of the women saw him standing by the stage and blew him a theatrical kiss. He felt his cheeks reddening.

Then he saw a couple of policemen walking through the crowd towards him and decided there was nothing for it but to level with them. He couldn't take much more of this. He approached them and said, 'I don't know who I am!'

The policemen looked at him, registered the collection of flyers he was holding and laughed out loud.

'Yeah, very good,' said one of the cops. 'But we're on duty. We haven't got time to take in a show.'

'I'm sure it's genius!' laughed the other cop.

'No, wait, you don't understand. I really...'

But they were already walking away and the moment was lost. The boy looked down at the sheaf of papers he was clutching and realised what had happened. He made a sound of disgust, hurried back to where he'd seen the litterbin and dumped the whole lot inside. The medieval wench saw him do it and gave him an indignant glare, so he turned away and moved back into the cover of the crowd, looking frantically around for somewhere he could sit down and get his thoughts together. He spotted a small clearing around a statue, a life-size figure of a man in old fashioned clothes and a top hat, so he went gratefully over to it and sat down on the statue's plinth, thinking he would just rest for a moment and get his breath back.

'Oi!' snapped a voice above him and he looked up in alarm to see that the 'statue' was glaring down at him. 'Get off me plinth! You'll damage it.'

The boy jumped up in alarm, realising that this wasn't a statue at all, just a man, painted grey from head to foot and wearing specially treated clothes. Even his plinth was just a painted wooden box.

'I'm sorry,' muttered the boy. 'I didn't realise you weren't… er… what… what are you doing?'

'Trying to make an honest living,' snarled the man in a broad Scottish accent. 'And you're not helping one wee bit!'

The boy heard laughter and turning, he saw that several passers-by had stopped to watch the proceedings, as though they thought it was all part of a show. One man was even lifting a camera to take a photograph. The boy turned back to the statue-man. 'I... I'm sorry, I thought you were *real*,' he stammered. He waved a hand around at the encircling magic. 'What... what is all this?' he asked.

'What's what?' snapped the statue-man.

'All these people...'

'It's the Festival,' snapped the statue. When the boy just stared up at him blankly, he added, 'The *Edinburgh* Festival. What did you think it was? Disneyland?'

'What's the... Edinburgh Festival?' asked the boy.

'It's three weeks of total madness,' said the statue-man. 'And a chance for me to earn enough money to see me through the winter. Now kindly stick some coins in the hat or sling your hook.'

'Oh, er...' The boy shoved a hand into his pocket, then realised he couldn't afford to give away the tiny bit of cash he had. 'Sorry, I... I can't really...'

'Let's have a photograph,' suggested the man with the camera, speaking in an American accent. Before the boy could even think about it, the statue reached down, grabbed him by the shoulder and pulled him in close. 'Smile,' hissed the statue-man in his ear and the boy did his best to comply, but the rictus grin he came up with couldn't have been very convincing.

The photographer stepped forward and dutifully dropped a coin into the statue-man's hat. 'Thanks, buddy,' he said.

'Thank you kindly, sir,' said the statue-man, doffing

his hat and then he pushed the boy away. 'Scram,' he said, none too politely.

The boy walked away, bewildered. He'd never heard of the Edinburgh Festival but had already decided that it was clearly an event intended for the insane. He scanned the way ahead, looking for somewhere quiet to hide himself but there didn't seem to be anywhere that fitted that description. He glanced hopefully through the open doors of shops and cafés but all them were rammed to the gills. He wandered down narrow side streets and had to double back when they proved to be impassable. Before very much longer, it dawned on him that it had actually been a bit quieter back where he'd started, so he retraced his steps, running the gamut of the leaflet distributors a second time, but refusing now to take any more flyers from them, keeping his hands in the pockets of his jeans.

He went back down the hill and as the afternoon faded into evening, he eventually found himself once again on Princes Street, walking alongside the park. Finding an empty wooden bench, he slumped down on it and sat, watching the world go by, trying to come up with some kind of plan but he could think of nothing that would be of any use. It occurred to him that perhaps he should try to find a police station, so he got up from the bench and asked several passers-by where he might find one, but every single person he spoke to had pretty much the same answer. 'Sorry, kid, I'm not from round here.' This was said in an American, an

Irish, a German and a French accent, before he finally gave up and went back to his bench. He felt completely exhausted by everything that had happened to him since he'd got off the train, so tired that he couldn't seem to think straight any more.

The hours passed steadily. Darkness descended, the streetlights came on and it didn't seem to be much quieter on the road than it had been in the day. Now it was dominated by large groups of young people hurrying off to one appointment or another, laughing and shouting to each other, taking no notice of the boy sitting alone on the bench. He started to wonder where he might sleep for the night and, on impulse, got up from the bench and went back through the entrance of the park, wondering if it stayed open all night. He was beginning to feel really tired.

He came to a place where a narrow cobbled path led upwards to a life-sized statue of a soldier on horseback, the horse standing on a tall rock plinth, the soldier gazing steadfastly out towards Princes Street. On the far side of the plinth, on a steep incline, there was a thickly-covered area of trees and shrubs. The boy paused for a closer look and noticed a narrow opening between the rows of foliage where somebody might be able to stretch himself out without being seen by passers-by. After glancing quickly around to ensure there was nobody observing him, he ducked under the metal rail that fenced the area off and crawled into the opening. The shrubs seemed to shrug around him like a blanket. He pulled up the hood of his jacket and lay on his side, listening to the sounds of the traffic passing by on the main road.

It was a strange lullaby but it worked well enough. Within minutes he was fast asleep.

THREE

Strange Encounter

It was the sound of a clock chiming that woke him, a deep echoing tone that he decided must be a church clock or something similar. He lay in the bushes, listening. It went on for a long time before it stopped and he wished he'd been able to count them, but for some reason, he decided it was probably midnight. Then he heard another noise, something unexpected and rather startling under the circumstances: a loud snort, followed by a whinny. It sounded, he thought, like a horse. But what would a horse be doing here in the middle of the night?

Cautiously, he lifted his head and peered out from the shrubs. The park, or at least, what he could see of it from his position next to the statue, appeared to be deserted. He became aware of a deep silence. There were no sounds of traffic from the main road, which seemed odd even at this late hour. Again, he heard the snorting and a weird clip-clopping noise.

'Huh?' He sat up, peering around in astonishment and now he heard a gruff voice from somewhere in the air above him, a voice that spoke with a strong Scottish accent.

'Steady on, Sultan, let's just take a wee moment to stretch ourselves!'

The boy stared up at the stone plinth rearing into the air above him. He was looking at something that he could scarcely believe. The statue of the horse was *moving* on its plinth, lifting its hooves and shaking its head. And then the boy saw that the soldier, sitting astride the horse, was also in motion, twisting his head this way and that, beneath his tall bearskin hat, and reaching out his arms as though having a much-needed stretch.

The boy got cautiously to his feet, telling himself that this guy was amazing. He made the statue-man he'd seen earlier look like an absolute beginner. How had he managed to stay still for so long? And how had he ever trained a horse to do it with him?' In standing up, the boy brushed against the vegetation and the soldier looked down at him.

'Halt! Who goes there?' he snapped.

'Er… it's just me,' said the boy, dismayed.

'Just *you*? Who's you?' growled the soldier. He studied the boy for a moment in astonishment. Then his eyes widened in evident surprise. 'You're a damned softie,' he said.

'Er… am I?' muttered the boy. 'What makes you say that?'

'I can *see* you are,' growled the soldier. 'Soft as anything.'

'Well that's not very nice,' said the boy. 'You've only just met me and you're calling me names!'

'I'm calling you what you so obviously are!' insisted the soldier. 'You're made of flesh and blood, boy. A softie. A *human.*' He pronounced the last word as though it was something despicable. 'Why aren't you asleep?'

'I was. But the sound of the clock woke me.' The boy looked around. 'Look, I'm sorry. If I'm spoiling your act, I'll find somewhere else to sleep.'

'My *act*?' The soldier gave a snort of derision. 'This is no act, Sonny Jim. This is a once a year occurrence. And what do you mean, "the clock woke you?" It's supposed to put you to sleep.'

'Is it?' The boy was completely confused. 'Well, I'm sorry, I was already asleep and the noise woke me up but… look, I'll leave you to it. I'm sorry, I can't afford to give you any money, but…'

'Money? Why would I want money?'

'Well, why else would you pretend to be a statue?'

'Hold on a minute,' said the soldier. 'I think you've got the wrong end of the stick, laddie.' He paused to pat his horse's flank. 'Sultan, get us down from here.'

As the boy stood watching in astonishment, the

horse lunged forward in an elegant leap, cleared the fence below and thudded down onto the sloping grass beyond it. He galloped on for a short distance, carried by his own momentum, then slowed, wheeled around and came trotting back up the cobbled path. The soldier halted the horse by the fence and sat there, studying the boy with interest. 'This is irregular,' he said, more to himself than to anyone else. 'Most irregular. I've never heard the like before.'

The boy didn't know what to say. Now he could see the soldier clearly in the moonlight, he began to feel afraid, because there was no costume on earth that could be *that* realistic. The man and his horse were clearly made of black metal, yet it was a metal that somehow moved at the joints as easily and smoothly as a human. As the boy stood there staring, the horse flared its nostrils and shook its head and every metal strand of its mane flowed and swayed as though made of real hair. The soldier was a foot or more bigger than any human had a right to be. He had a fierce, proud face, his top lip adorned with a thick moustache and the eyes that appraised the boy, despite also being made of metal, were keen and sparkled with intelligence. The boy couldn't help but notice one odd detail. The soldier's tall hat was liberally peppered with long white streaks. 'I'm Colonel Robert Macintosh Alexander,' he announced grandly. 'My friends call me... The Colonel. Now you'd better do a bit of explaining. Who are you, lad?'

Good question. The boy shook his head. 'I er… this is going to sound a bit odd,' he said.

'Yes?' said the Colonel, expectantly.

'I umm… well, I don't know *who* I am.'

There was a long silence.

'Come now,' said the Colonel. 'You must surely know who you are? Everyone knows that much.'

'But I don't,' said the boy. 'I don't know anything. I guess it sounds weird, but… well, all I know is I woke up on a train just as it was arriving at the station over there…' The boy pointed in the general direction of Edinburgh Waverley. 'And since then, I've been wandering around Edinburgh trying to remember stuff. Except that I can't seem to come up with anything at all. Anyway, then I got tired so I lay down here in the bushes. And the next thing I knew, your horse made a loud noise and…'

'Ah yes, that's Sultan for you, always eager to get moving. As soon as the bell wakes him, he… well, he *has* been waiting all year.'

The boy laughed. 'This is nuts,' he said. 'It's barmy. I'm standing here talking to a flipping statue!'

'Yes, and very privileged you are to be doing so,' said the Colonel. 'I don't think there's ever been a softie… er, I mean a human that's been afforded that honour in all the years the Calling has taken place.'

'The… Calling?'

'That's our name for it,' said the Colonel, smiling with evident pride. 'From midnight, August the

21

second, to midnight, August the third. The Calling is the one night of the year where we all come together to celebrate who we are. Twenty-four hours of total freedom, with not a single softie in sight.' The Colonel frowned. 'Until now, that is. Oh dear. I don't know what Charlie will have to say about this.'

'Charlie?'

The Colonel ignored the boy's question. 'I suppose we'll have to go and talk to him. Unless of course, you could see your way to just... going back to sleep and letting us get on with things?'

The boy frowned. 'I don't really think I *could* sleep now,' he said. 'I'm not tired. And there's too much going on.'

'I was afraid you'd say that. What made you choose my particular patch to have your nap?'

'Umm... well, it was just because there were all these bushes.'

'Bushes. I see. It wasn't because of any particular interest in the Royal Scots Greys, then?'

'The what?'

'The Royal Scots Greys.' The Colonel waved a gloved hand at the plinth, where the boy now noticed a large metal plaque. 'The glorious regiment that I was put here to commemorate. No, of course not. You'll know nothing of our illustrious history... our famous charge against Napoleon at Waterloo... our noble endeavours in the Boer War!'

'Umm... no, sorry... is that a problem?'

'No. Typical is what that is. Softies go past me day after day and how many of them know or even *care* why I'm here? Oh no, I'm just a photo opportunity. Me, in the foreground, with the castle behind me. Oh, if I only had a guinea for every photograph that's been taken! The favourite shot, of course, is when there's a blasted seagull perched on my head.'

'Oh, is that what all the white stuff is?' The boy grimaced. 'Not nice.'

'You've no idea. If I could move on a normal day, I'd twist their ruddy necks for them! Sometimes I swear they do it just for mischief! And you softies are no better. If one more idiot climbs up here and sticks a traffic cone on my bonce, I'll not be responsible for my actions!'

'So you… you *can* see, then? I mean, on normal days.'

'Of course I can see. We can *all* see. We just can't move.' The Colonel seemed to ponder for a moment, then seemed to reach a decision. 'Well, we can't stand here chatting all night,' he said. 'I've got things to organise.' He leaned forward in his saddle and extended a gloved hand. 'You'd best climb up behind me,' he said. 'And we'll see what's to be done about you.'

After a moment's hesitation, the boy took the Colonel's hand. It was the strangest feeling. The hand was metal sure enough, but it was somehow soft and yielding, as though it was actually alive. The Colonel was clearly very strong. He pulled hard and lifted the boy clear of the ground and up over the fence, then swung him expertly around and dropped him onto the saddle behind him, making Sultan skitter momentarily. Even the metal saddle beneath the boy felt surprisingly comfortable.

'Whoah, Sultan, easy now.' The Colonel clicked his tongue and Sultan moved away from the fence and started walking down the cobbled track to the flat grass beyond.

'*I'm still asleep and dreaming this*,' the boy decided. How else was he to explain it? And yet he had never had a dream so detailed, so utterly convincing as this one. What other explanation was there? Madness? Was he insane?

The Colonel guided Sultan in the direction of the park entrance. 'So,' he said, 'you know nothing about yourself. I think the condition is called amnesia. I knew a chappie once who suffered from the very same thing. He was my batman, actually.'

'Batman?' echoed the boy. That seemed to ring a bell somewhere in his head. He had a momentary vision of a cloaked figure in a black mask, but the Colonel ignored his question and carried on talking. 'He fought alongside me in Pretoria. A shell exploded beside him at the Battle of Diamond Hill and he was never the same again.'

'I'm… sorry to hear that,' said the boy. It seemed like the kind of thing he ought to say.

'Oh, don't be sorry, he was a bit of an idiot to tell you

the truth. Always put sugar in my tea, even though I told him repeatedly I took it without. After his accident, he wasn't even capable of making tea. Used to just sit there and whistle all the time. A music hall song. *The Boy I Love is Up in the Gallery*. Damned annoying, really.' The Colonel twisted his head slightly. 'I don't suppose *you've* been close to an explosion?' he ventured.

'I… don't think so.'

'Well, it's a mystery sure enough and one that will need to be properly investigated.'

They were approaching the long flight of steps up to the road, but Sultan took them easily in his stride. As they neared the top, the boy saw that another tall metal statue was waiting on the far side of the closed gates. He raised a hand and waved to the Colonel.

'Hello there!'

'Ah, good evening, David. Good of you to wait for me.'

As they drew closer, the boy saw that the statue was of a middle-aged man. He was dressed in a jacket with what looked like a cloak slung over one shoulder. Like the Colonel, he had a thick moustache and a pair of sideburns. He wore stout walking boots and for some reason was holding a book in one hand. On a thick belt around his waist he wore some kind of a purse and a pistol.

'Everything all right?' asked David. He was studying the boy with some bemusement. 'I say,' he muttered. 'Isn't that a… softie riding behind you?'

The Colonel pulled Sultan to a halt.

'I'm afraid so. I'd introduce you to him but it's not as simple as you might suppose. He doesn't seem to know who he is.'

'That's odd.' David smiled up at the boy. 'I've never seen a softie at the Calling before,' he said.

'That's because it's never happened,' said the Colonel. 'Not in my memory, anyway. It's hard to know what to do for the best. I thought I'd take him along to see Charlie.'

David raised his eyebrows. 'Is that wise?' he asked.

'Well, I can't think of a better course of action. Of course, Charlie will *love* all the attention.'

'Won't he just?' David chuckled. 'We'll surely have to call the lad something,' he said. He studied the boy for a moment. 'He looks like an Edward to me.' He smiled. 'And since he's turned up in our fair city, why don't we just call him Ed for short?'

'Ed Fest?' suggested the Colonel and both statues chuckled. Then David smiled at the boy and said, 'Pleased to meet you, young man. I'm David Livingstone.' Then he stretched out a huge hand to shake.

FOUR

David

Ed was delighted to realise that here, finally, was a name he actually recognised. 'David Livingstone, the explorer?' he asked.

David smiled with evident pleasure and glanced at the Colonel. 'Ah, you see, there's still one or two who remember me!'

'Lucky you,' muttered the Colonel ungraciously.

'I read about you,' said Ed excitedly. 'At... school, I think. You... you were the one who spent all those years in Africa.'

'That's me,' agreed David. 'I was actually searching for the source of the Nile. Never found it though. Discovered a whole bunch of lakes instead. And I also discovered other things – malaria, cholera and dysentery to name but three.'

'Countries?' asked Ed.

'Tropical illnesses,' said David. 'I had all three of them at one time or another. I'm afraid that's why I never made it back to my homeland.' He opened the book he was holding. Ed saw that it was hollow inside and contained a bunch of keys. David took them out, selected one, slotted it into the lock on the gate and turned it with a loud click. Then he swung the gate open, allowing the Colonel to ride through.

'I'll leave it open for now,' said David. 'There's sure to be a few stragglers back there.' He nodded to an empty podium away to their right. 'I see Allan has already made his escape. Must have jumped clear over the fence!'

'Allan?' murmured Ed.

'Allan Ramsay,' elaborated the Colonel. 'You've heard of *him*?'

'Is he a footballer?' ventured Ed and once again, the two statues laughed.

'Oh, he'd love to hear that,' said David. 'No, he's a poet. A playwright…'

'And a wigmaker,' added the Colonel mysteriously.

David returned the key to the hollow book and closed it. 'I suppose we'd better go and release Wally?' he suggested. 'Or perhaps we should give him a miss this year?'

'Are you kidding? We'd never hear the last of it,' said the Colonel. 'Come on, you know we have to.'

They crossed the road and started along Princes

Street. A couple of cars were parked at the traffic lights, their headlights on, but inside them, the drivers seemed curiously still.

The Colonel chuckled. 'The boy thought I was pretending to be a statue,' he said. 'Got me mixed up with one of those blasted street-performers.'

David made a face. 'Oh, that lot,' he growled. 'Amateurs!'

'How they've got the cheek to call themselves statues is beyond me,' said the Colonel. 'I've seen them on this very road. It's all they can do to stand still for five minutes.'

'I saw quite a good one today,' said Ed. 'Well, he fooled me, anyway.'

'That's not saying much,' said the Colonel. 'No offence, lad, but you don't strike me as being particularly bright.'

'Go easy on the boy,' advised David. 'This must all seem strange to him.'

'You can say that again,' muttered Ed. 'I'm still not sure this is really happening.'

'Oh, trust me,' said the Colonel. 'It's happening. It shouldn't be, but it is.'

'So, I'm not dreaming?'

'No,' said David. 'Trust us, you're wide awake.'

They continued on their way along Princes Street and it suddenly occurred to Ed how eerily quiet it was. There was no traffic moving at all, but now he noticed a couple more cars actually parked on the road, as though they'd suddenly stopped dead in mid journey, the drivers all slumped asleep behind the wheel. Then they passed a bus, the windows brightly lit up and Ed could see that several seats were occupied by sleeping people. Sultan came level with the cab and there was the driver, upright at the steering wheel, his head drooping slightly, his shoulders rising and falling, his eyes closed. Ed began to understand what the Colonel had said earlier.

'So… most people fall asleep when the clock strikes twelve?' he asked.

'Not most people,' said the Colonel. '*All* people. Everyone, that is, but you.'

'It's a wonder there aren't accidents,' said Ed.

'Oh, it's very cleverly done,' said David. He gestured at the bus. 'You see, at midnight on the 2nd of August, human time in Edinburgh simply ceases to exist. Automobiles stop dead in their tracks. Engines simply stop operating. People fall asleep exactly as they are.' He pointed to a man standing at a bus stop just ahead of them, a thick-set fellow in a raincoat, his hands shoved in his pockets. As they came closer, Ed saw that the man's eyes were shut. He was fast asleep, but somehow still upright. 'Weird,' he said.

'They know nothing of the situation,' continued David. 'Of course, most people will simply sleep through the whole experience at home in their beds. But those who do not, well, at midnight tomorrow, they'll open their eyes and think they've simply blinked for an instant. The engines of their automobiles will start to run again and life will go on just as before. This is the miracle of the Calling.'

'But… don't they notice that they've lost a day?' reasoned Ed.

'No, because they haven't actually lost anything. You see, the Calling slots in between the two days. It exists in a separate dimension entirely. In the softie world, that whole twenty-four hours passes in the blink of an eye. But for us, it runs in real time.' He made a gesture of exasperation. 'I wish James was here. He'd be able to explain it much better than I.'

'James?'

'James Clerk Maxwell. Famous Edinburgh physicist. He's the only one of us who really understands how it works.'

'Mind you, he is a bit of a genius,' said The Colonel.

'Is he?'

'Oh yes,' said David. 'Everyone knows that Albert Einstein couldn't have come up with his famous theory without James' discoveries.'

Einstein, thought Ed. Another name he thought he recognised.

'So that's… the theory of relativity, right?'

'Absolutely.' David glanced at the Colonel. 'Maybe he's not so dim after all. Did I get it about right, by the way? The explanation?'

The Colonel chuckled. 'I've never understood it,' he admitted. "But I'm just a simple military man. I prefer to think of it as magic. All I know is, it happens and I'm very grateful for it.'

'Hmm.' David shrugged. 'Well anyway, we might see James around later.' He glanced at Ed. 'He has a statue too.'

'Yes, but he's a blow-in,' said the Colonel. 'Didn't get his until 2008.'

'When was yours?' asked Ed.

'Me? 1906,' said the Colonel, proudly, as though he'd rehearsed it.

Ed looked at David. 'And you?'

'1875 to 1876.'

Ed raised his eyebrows. 'What took so long?' he asked.

'The artist was a bit too leisurely for her own good,' said David. 'Kept breaking off to work on other things. Most frustrating.'

They were approaching a huge stone monument a short distance into the upper level of the gardens, a kind of arch with three pointed spires that reared up into the night sky. Sitting beneath the arch was the huge white stone figure of a man, draped in a cloak. Ed noticed that he had a large dog at his side, which he was stroking affectionately. As the group drew nearer, he turned his head and looked down at them. 'Ah, good evening, gentlemen,' he said. 'I thought you'd never get here. Now, hurry up and get this gate unlocked. It's time for the night's festivities to begin!'

FIVE

Sir Walter

David opened his hollow book and took out the keys. He inserted one into the lock and opened the gate. The white statue got to his feet and came down the steps of the monument, walking with a pronounced limp. Now Ed could appreciate exactly how big he was – perhaps three times life size.

'Wow, you're huge!' exclaimed Ed and the statue stopped in its tracks and stared down at him, his stone eyebrows raised.

'Is somebody going to explain this apparition?' he asked.

'Ah, well now, Walter…' began the Colonel.

'That's *Sir* Walter, if you please,' snapped the man. The dog had followed him down the stairs, but he turned and snapped a command. 'No, Maida, stay here and guard the tripod,' he said. The dog, a huge skinny thing, gave a disappointed whimper and slunk back up the steps, looking extremely sorry for himself. Sir Walter turned back to the Colonel. 'Well?' he asked.

'Umm… yes, well, you see I woke up as usual and there was this young softie just standing there, looking up at me.'

'Why wasn't he asleep?'

'I really don't know. It is unique in my experience. I'm wondering if it's something to do with the fact that he's lost his memory. Maybe the usual rules just don't apply to amnesiacs.'

'Curious.' Sir Walter came closer, looming over Sultan and his two riders. He inspected Ed at close range, the expression on his big face suggesting he didn't much like what he was looking at. He had a large forehead and his curly hair was cut in a sort of short fringe. Ed noticed that Sir Walter too was carrying a book. 'To answer your impertinent question, my lad, yes, I *am* big. But no bigger than my legend demands.' He jerked a thumb over his shoulder. 'That, my boy, is the Scott Monument and it is the biggest monument in Edinburgh. It is over two hundred feet tall and cost more than sixteen thousand pounds to build, which, let me assure you, was a pretty penny back in the 1840s. The construction took over four years to complete.'

As he spoke, Ed was aware of David beside him, rolling his eyes. Sir Walter didn't seem to notice and continued loudly.

'It is possibly the biggest monument ever dedicated to the memory of a writer,' he said.

'Oh, you're a writer?' muttered Ed.

Sir Walter looked affronted. He actually took a step back. 'Of course I'm a writer, ' he said. 'Did you not pick up the clues, boy? Were you not listening?' He leaned close again. 'Sir. Walter. Scott.' He said the three words slowly, as though speaking to an idiot, and when this prompted no reaction, he added, 'You've heard of me, of course?'

Ed frowned. He wanted to shake his head, but was afraid to.

'He's heard of *me*,' muttered David, but Sir Walter ignored the taunt.

'It must be because he's lost his memory,' he said. He looked Ed directly in the eyes and prompted him. 'I mean, everyone's heard of me!' He glared at Ed. 'The author of such literary classics as *The Heart of Midlothian?*'

No reaction.

'*Ivanhoe?*'

Again nothing.

'*The Peveril of the Peak?*'

This last title seemed to strike a chord with Ed. There *was* a familiar ring to it. Sir Walter must have noticed his look because he smiled triumphantly. 'Of course, *everyone's* read that book,' he said. 'It's a classic.' But in Ed's mind, this was nothing to do with a book. There was a fleeting but vivid image of a green doorway and a dark green sign above that door with those same words written on it. The sign was set against a tiled wall of a paler green. Then he saw, quite clearly, a man going in through the doorway and the door swinging shut behind him. The vision was only there for an instant and it was gone as suddenly as it had appeared, but a powerful conviction remained in Ed's mind. This was a place he knew, a place he had seen in real life.

'*The Peveril of the Peak*,' he muttered.

'Yes?' said Sir Walter, expectantly.

'Isn't that... isn't it a pub?'

Sir Walter couldn't have looked more offended if he'd tried. 'A pub?' he cried. 'How dare you? You're speaking of one of the greatest masterpieces ever written. A pub indeed!' He looked accusingly at the Colonel. 'I'm holding you responsible for this,' he said. 'You brought him along.'

'Well, what else was I supposed to do with him?' asked the Colonel.

'Couldn't you have... drawn your sabre and dispatched him?'

'He's a wee boy!' protested the Colonel.

'And a very ignorant one,' said Sir Walter, flatly. 'Well, be it on your own head. I don't know what Charlie will have to say about it.'

'I don't really understand,' said Ed and the three statues looked at him in surprise.

'What don't you understand?' asked the Colonel, half turning in his saddle.

'Well, I'm not being funny…'

'I can assure you, none of us are laughing,' said Sir Walter.

'But… you guys are just statues of famous people, right?'

All three of them nodded.

'So, you're not really Colonel Alexander… and he's not really David Livingstone.' He turned his head. 'And you're not really Sir William Scott.'

'Sir *Walter* Scott!'

'Er… sorry! Yes… you're just statues of them. But you all talk as though you really *are* them, so…'

'Don't you know anything?' muttered Sir Walter. 'Are you really that stupid? When an artist creates a statue, the spirit of the person the statue represents enters into the stone or the bronze or whatever it happens to be made of. It becomes an embodiment of everything that they ever knew or did. I should have thought that was obvious.'

Ed winced. 'Sorry, I didn't know.'

'Well you know now,' growled Sir Walter. 'And you'd do well to memorise the fact, before you go making a fool of yourself again.'

'Erm… right. Sorry.'

'Well,' said Sir Walter, 'we've wasted enough time talking to this urchin. Shall we be on our way?'

The other two statues nodded. The Colonel clicked his tongue and urged Sultan on along the street at a sedate walk. Ed couldn't see the Colonel's face but he noticed that David was trying very hard not to laugh, something that suggested he found Sir Walter every bit as pompous as Ed did.

They travelled onwards through the heart of the neon-lit city. They came to a set of railings that was hung with a row of brightly coloured posters.

'All these things,' said Ed, pointing to them. 'They're like shows that you can go and see?'

'Yes,' said Sir Walter, disdainfully. 'It's what passes for entertainment these days.' He indicated the grinning face of a man. 'Look at that oaf. A so-called comedian. That's what this city is best known for now. Gurning fools who stand up on the stage with the sole intent of making people laugh. And idiots come from all across the globe to see them. They actually pay money for the privilege.' He shook his head. 'I don't know what the world is coming to,' he said.

'Oh, a good laugh isn't so bad, surely?' said David.

'But what about culture?' asked Sir Walter. 'What about intellectual debate? Once upon a time people were happy to lose themselves in a good book.'

'They still are,' reasoned Ed. 'What about J K Rowling?' He gasped, realising that he'd just come up with something else that he somehow knew. Yes! J K Rowling, the author of the Harry Potter books. He *knew* this. He didn't know *how* he knew it, but he knew it just the same.

'She's an Edinburgh girl,' said the Colonel.

'Oh, wow. Has she got a statue?'

'Not yet,' said Sir Walter, 'but it's probably only a matter of time. Most of us have to die before they'll consider doing one, but no doubt they'll make an exception for *her*.'

Ed considered what he'd just learned. He knew an author's name and he knew the books that she'd written, so, he assumed, he must have read them back in his everyday life, wherever that was. Maybe, given a little time, he'd remember more things, things that might help him to remember who he was.

They continued on their way. Every so often they passed the occasional human asleep in some strange posture, but there weren't that many people around. Halfway up the hill, they came across a group of young men who had stopped in mid-walk on the pavement, obliging Ed and his companions to move into the road to get past them. They were all standing, their arms raised, their mouths open as though they'd been yelling at each other when the clock struck, but every one of them now had his eyes closed. Ed noticed that each man was wearing a red t-shirt with a bright yellow slogan printed on it. '*The Groom*,' read one. '*The Best Man*,' read another, while others simply had a series of nicknames printed on them – *The Rooster*, *Six Dinner Sam* and *Billy Boy* were amongst the ones that Ed noticed.

'A stag party,' muttered the Colonel, sounding faintly disgusted. 'There seem to be more of them every year. Giving our proud city a bad name.'

'Oh, they're just letting off steam,' said David. 'I don't mind them myself.'

'If you don't mind me saying, Mr Livingstone, you have a very liberal attitude,' said Sir Walter. 'Some might say, too liberal by half.' He made an effort to change the subject. 'Are you two entering the Agon?' he asked.

David frowned. 'I thought I might give it a miss,' he said. 'My talk about the lakes of Africa didn't seem to go down too well last year.'

'Oh, you're being modest,' said Sir Walter. 'I spoke with one or two people afterwards who claimed to have found it… quite diverting.'

'I've been mulling over another epic poem,' said the Colonel. 'About the Scots Greys' charge…'

'You did that last year,' interrupted Sir Walter. 'Sounded a bit too much like the *Charge of the Light Brigade* for comfort.'

'No, that one was about our charge at the Battle of Diamond Hill,' said the Colonel. 'This one would be about our charge at the Battle of Fontenoy, during the War of Austrian Succession.'

Sir Walter scowled. 'But that would surely have been before your time,' he complained.

'Well, I've used my imagination,' said the Colonel. 'To be honest, one epic charge is much like another. A whole lot of galloping. And you're not telling me you have personal experience of the kind of jousting that takes place in *Ivanhoe?*'

'Fair point, well made,' said Sir Walter. 'I myself have composed an ode to the city of Edinburgh itself. I'm rather pleased with it. It's thirty-four verses long. I'm fairly confident of winning the tripod again. Obviously, over the year I've memorised it in its entirety. If you gentlemen would care to hear a few verses, I'd be more than happy…'

'The Agon is a competition,' said David hastily. He was pretending to speak for Ed's benefit, but Ed was fairly certain he was just trying to get out of listening to Sir Walter's poem. 'We statues hold it every year. It's named after a Classic Greek tradition. It's for poetry and oratory in general.'

'And… the tripod?'

'That's the prize,' said David. 'It's actually kept up in the Scott Monument, but each year it's awarded to whoever is judged the best performer.'

'I win it most years,' said Sir Walter, with stunning immodesty. 'The tripod is a replica of a prize given in 334 BC at the theatre of Dionysus in Greece. Obviously, on the rare occasions that somebody else wins it, it cannot be taken away, but it is awarded symbolically. It's very valuable.'

'Is that why you left your dog to guard it?' asked Ed.

'Absolutely. One cannot be too careful. Most of the older statues are completely trustworthy but some of the more contemporary fellows have a more cavalier attitude to property.' Sir Walter paused for a moment and the Colonel pulled Sultan to a halt. 'Well, if you gentlemen will excuse me, I think I'll go and pay a visit to the University,' said Sir Walter. 'I like to see if there's anything new going on in my old stamping ground.'

'Are you all right for a key?' asked David.

Sir Walter smiled and opened the book he'd been carrying, revealing that it too was hollow and held a selection of keys. 'I'm going to pop into the library,' he said. 'See who's been reading me. And…' He leaned closer. 'I'm going to google myself. It's fascinating to read what people are still saying about me after all these years.' He gave Ed a proud look. 'Last year was my one hundred and twentieth anniversary, you know. You should have seen the tributes!' He turned away. 'Well, see you at the Agon!'

With that he limped off across the road, looking freakishly big as he walked past a parked car. The Colonel clicked his tongue and they moved on in silence for some distance, David occasionally checking to see where Sir Walter was. Once he had gone down a side street, out of sight, David let out a long breath and said, 'What a big-headed braggart!'

The Colonel chuckled. 'He always *did* have a high opinion of himself,' he agreed. 'Mind you, to be fair, he does write rather well.'

'I'm not saying he doesn't,' protested David. 'It's just that he likes the sound of his own voice a little too much.'

'Why is he limping?' asked Ed.

David looked awkward. 'Oh, I... believe he had polio when he was a nipper. Terrible thing, really.'

'But... a statue can't have polio, surely?'

'True,' admitted David. 'But it's like he told you. We take on all the attributes of the person we're commemorating. So if the man limped in real life, so will his statue. You'll get used to the idea.'

Ed was about to ask something else but he broke off when he saw something weird approaching along the street, racing down the middle of the road. At a distance it looked like two real giraffes but as they drew nearer, he could see that they were actually made of lengths of black metal that had been bolted together. One was a couple of feet shorter than the other, and both had empty spaces in the middle of their necks, but it didn't seem to be slowing them down at all. They went racing down the hill, their metal hooves striking sparks on the tarmac, their wire cable tails flicking from side to side.

'Dreaming Spires,' said David.

Ed looked at him. 'Huh?' he said.

'That's what they're called, apparently. They're usually located up on Leith Walk. Fancy name, but I'd say they are of fairly limited intelligence. It's the same every year. When the clock strikes, they just go mad and make a run for it.'

'One year, one of them went straight into an automobile,' said the Colonel. 'Made a great big dent in it. I don't know how anyone explained that one away.'

'So it's every statue in the city?' asked Ed.

'Yes, every single one. Oh, you'll see some wonders tonight, that I can promise you. Assuming, of course, that Charlie allows you to stay.'

Ed frowned. 'Who *is* this Charlie you keep talking about?' he asked.

'You'll find out soon enough,' said the Colonel. 'We're almost there.'

'Where's that?' Ed asked him.

'Parliament Square,' said David.

SIX

Please To See The King!

As they approached the square, it quickly became apparent that an awful lot of statues had already made their way there. The Colonel turned Sultan off the main road and they entered the square itself, which was absolutely packed with stone and metal figures of varying sizes. They were all jostling to get a clearer view of the black metal figure of a man on horseback, posed on a central plinth. Behind him was a huge building that featured rows of stone columns. The mounted man was gazing fiercely down at the crowds around him and occasionally shouting instructions to them in a plummy English accent.

'That's decided then,' Ed heard him say. He pointed into the crowd. 'You two will lead the procession and you three will carry the flags.' He pointed to another area. 'Do you think you could find some musicians to accompany them? You can? Good, excellent.'

'Is that Charlie?' asked Ed and both the Colonel and David gave him warning glares.

'Keep your voice down!' hissed David. 'You don't want him to hear you calling him that.'

'But... that's what *you* call him,' protested Ed.

'Never to his face,' said the Colonel. 'If he speaks to you, you call him 'Your Majesty'. Got that?'

'OK, whatever you say... so who is he exactly?' whispered Ed. 'He *looks* like a Roman soldier or something.'

'Whatever you do, don't mention that!' David told him. 'He's never been happy about it. He's King Charles the Second and he's been here longer than any of us, so his word is law. But his sculptor had some ridiculous notion of making him look like a Roman centurion, and of course, that can't be changed now. So, mind you don't...'

He broke off as he realised that several of the statues ranged in front of them had started glancing back over their shoulders and were staring at Ed in evident amazement. As each statue became aware of his presence, they prodded the statues next to them, who also turned their heads and after a few moments, audible gasps of astonishment began to be heard. The effect rippled through the crowd like a wave and a general buzz of conversation rose up. It wasn't long before Charlie became aware that something was going on.

'What's happening down there?' he demanded. 'You lot need to pay attention when your king is… oh!' Now he had seen the little human figure leaning out to look past the Colonel. 'Oh my golly gosh!' said Charlie. 'What in the name of…? Is that what I think it is?'

'It's a softie!' cried a voice from the crowd and this was quickly followed by a chorus of similar shouts. Ed looked around apprehensively. None of the faces that were staring at him looked particularly friendly. 'What's he doing here?' shrieked a high-pitched voice and then, worryingly, someone else bellowed. 'Get him! Bash him up!'

There was a sudden commotion and for an instant, it looked as though several statues were going to turn on Ed and drag him off Sultan's back. But the Colonel reached to his belt, pulled out his pistol and fired a shot into the air. The loud bang echoed around the square and made every statue freeze in its tracks.

'Just hold on a wee moment!' shouted the Colonel, sounding surprisingly calm under the circumstances. 'Let's not do anything hasty.' He gazed defiantly around, looking for opposition, and when he found none, he turned his gaze towards the central plinth. 'Please excuse my actions, Your Majesty, but I think the lad deserves a fair hearing before we do anything rash.'

Charlie scowled down at the Colonel, his expression decidedly cross. 'Discharging a pistol in Parliament Square?' he growled. 'Whatever next? A cannon?' He waved a hand. 'Really, Colonel Alexander, you go too far!'

'A thousand apologies, Your Majesty.'

Charlie sighed, but seemed to relent. 'Approach,' he told the Colonel. 'You too, Dr Livingstone. I'm absolutely agog to hear your explanation for this outrage.'

As if by magic, the sea of statues moved to the left and right and a narrow avenue appeared, leading directly to the plinth. The Colonel and David glanced at each other in evident apprehension. Then the Colonel clicked his tongue and urged Sultan gently forward. David walked by his side. Ed glanced nervously from side to side and saw to his concern that every pair of eyes around him appeared to be full of suspicion. Sultan finally came to a halt a short distance from the plinth and Ed looked up into the king's equally baleful glare.

'Er... good evening, your... Your Majesty!' he said and an astonished gasp rose from the crowd, as though none of them had realised that humans could actually speak. 'It's... very nice to meet you.'

'Very nice? It's more than very nice!' said Charlie with evident disgust. 'It's an honour, boy, one that has never been offered to a softie before, not in living history. Very nice, indeed!' He looked at the Colonel. 'Well?' he said. 'I'm waiting.'

'Your Majesty, this young lad appears to be suffering from amnesia,' said the Colonel. 'My theory is that this is why the usual way of things didn't apply to him.

When the clock chimed, instead of falling asleep, he…
well, he woke up. I really didn't think I should leave
him wandering around Edinburgh observing what was
going on, so naturally, I brought him to you.'

'You did the right thing,' said Charles. 'Although I
have to tell you, I do not approve of you discharging a
firearm in my presence.' He scowled. 'The question is,
now the boy *is* here, what's to be done with him? It's
dashed awkward.' He looked thoughtful for a moment.
'I suppose I could simply order his execution…'

Ed looked desperately around. He didn't much like
the sound of this.

'Hang on a minute!' he cried. 'That's not fair!'

Again, there was a gasp from the crowd.

'Hold your tongue,' snapped Charlie. 'It's not for
you to comment on my deliberations. Are you aware
of who I am?'

'Er… yes, your… Your Majesty but… you can't just
go around giving orders like that. This isn't my fault.'

'Not your fault, indeed! Pray then, tell me who's
fault it is.'

'Er… I don't… I can't…'

David chose this moment to interrupt. 'It would
seem a very rash course of action to execute the boy,
Your Majesty. We've had the opportunity to indulge in
a good chat with him on the way here and he seems a
nice enough sort…'

'A bit simple, perhaps,' added the Colonel. 'Not the
brightest, but then that's only typical of the softie race.'

'Er… quite,' said David. 'And being so young, it would seem very severe to… you know…' He made a chopping motion with one hand.

Charlie sniffed. 'It was good enough for my father,' he observed.

'Yes, but that too was a tragedy,' continued David. 'And you know the old saying, "two wrongs don't make a right"? I wouldn't be in a great hurry to go along that road, Your Majesty. I mean, a grown man would be one thing, but a helpless young boy?'

'Hmm. Well, I'm not suggesting I would undertake such an action lightly. But I do worry that he has witnessed something that was not meant for his eyes.'

David continued. 'I feel, Your Majesty, that this would be a rare opportunity for us to learn more about these strange, elusive creatures. We may already observe them from our plinths on a daily basis, but when have we ever had the chance to study them properly, to converse with them, to ask them questions?'

'Hmm.' Charlie seemed to be considering the point. 'I see what you're driving at, Dr Livingstone, but…'

'Might I also be so bold as to remind Your Majesty that in your lifetime you were often referred to as "the Merry Monarch?" It wouldn't sit well with your image, would it, if you condemned a young, helpless lad to death?'

Charlie narrowed his eyes. 'Allow *me* to worry about my image, Dr Livingstone,' he said. 'The idiot artist who decided to portray me as a Roman soldier clearly didn't give the subject very much thought.' He turned his gaze to Ed. 'Well, what say you, boy? Can you think of any good reason why I should be inclined to be merciful?'

Ed swallowed hard. 'Well...' he said. 'I... I didn't ask to be here. I just woke up on a train as it was arriving and well, here I am. I don't know anything. I... I don't even know my own name!'

A murmur went up from the crowd at this point. It sounded, Ed thought, fairly sympathetic.

'We've named him Ed,' interrupted the Colonel, trying to be helpful, but a warning glare from the monarch shut him up.

'I promise,' continued Ed, 'that I will never... *ever* tell anyone about what's happened here, cross my heart and hope to... to...' He broke off, not much liking the direction this was taking. 'I... I think it's really cool, by the way.'

'Cool?' snapped Charlie. 'It's August!'

'No, I mean it's great, you know, seeing all this and being allowed to be a part of it. It's like... really fantastic. The Colonel here and Dr Livingstone, they've been like, really helpful, and I even met Sir William Scott...'

'Walter!' hissed the Colonel.

'Yes, Sir Walter Scott and he was... well, he was dead nice too, once I got used to him. He helped explain how it all works, you know, the Calling and he told me all about his monument and how much it cost and everything…'

'Now why doesn't that surprise me?' muttered Charlie.

'So, I hope… I hope you'll be OK with me being here and give me like a chance to, you know, get my head together and work out who I really am, so I can go home again… where… wherever that is.'

There was a long, tense silence, before Charlie said, 'Well, I think I followed *most* of that.' He looked around at the mass of statues below him. 'I'm still of the opinion that we should ensure the boy doesn't have the opportunity to tell any other softies what he has seen here. I say we should execute him!' Another cheer went up from the crowd and Ed's stomach turned a somersault. This wasn't going well, he decided. This wasn't going well at all.

SEVEN

The Vote

There was a brief silence and then David stepped away from Sultan and strode decisively forward to stand at the very foot of Charlie's plinth. He turned to face the crowd, scanning the rows of faces.

'So, our king speaks out for execution,' he roared. 'But this is the twenty-first century. So why don't we put it to the vote?' He looked up at Charles. 'Democracy is very popular these days and I'm sure Your Majesty would wish to bow to the times?'

Charles looked aghast. 'Well, I…'

'Very good, Your Majesty, I thought you'd see it that way!' David turned his face back to the crowd. 'Statues of Edinburgh!' he said. 'Let me hear your thoughts on this matter. Who thinks the innocent young boy should forfeit his life for this transgression?'

A great roar went up from the crowd and Ed's heart nearly stopped beating in his chest.

'Oh dear,' he heard the Colonel mutter.

David waited until the yells and whoops had died down, then he looked hopefully around the assembly again. 'And... who would prefer to be enlightened and merciful? Who says he should be allowed to live?'

Another cheer went up and though the Colonel yelled as enthusiastically as he could, it was horribly clear to Ed that the first cheer had been by far the loudest. He felt his blood turning to ice in his veins. This wasn't looking promising. Once again David waited for the last sounds to die away before he spoke. 'It would seem that unlike recent historical events in this city, the 'Yes' vote has been the most vociferous. And so, this young lad is to face the ultimate penalty. The king has spoken and his subjects have spoken. His Majesty shall need then, one man from amongst you to step forward and actually perform the execution. Now... which of you shall it be?'

There was a long, long silence. Ed held his breath and hoped for the best.

'Oh, come along,' urged David, walking backwards and forwards at the base of the plinth, gazing at the crowd as he did so. 'You all seemed so keen to have him despatched. Which one of you will volunteer for the job?'

Another silence.

'Surely one of you?'

An even longer silence.

'Somebody? *Anybody*?'

Not one statue seemed prepared to step forward. David turned his head to look at Ed and gave him a tight-lipped smile, before continuing. 'Funny, isn't it, that so many of us are happy to bellow our demands? And yet, when it comes to action, so few are prepared to back them up with deeds. And lucky for you, boy, that this city has never commissioned a statue of any of its famous executioners.' He turned and lifted his gaze to the king. 'It would appear, Your Majesty, that nobody is prepared to take the boy's life. Unless of course, you'd be prepared to do it personally?'

Charles looked down at David, a glare of anger on his face. 'I?' he growled. 'The king? Reduced to the role of a common executioner? I really don't think so!'

'In that case, Your Majesty, I would suggest that your only option is to pardon him.'

Charles narrowed his eyes and shook his head. 'You go too far, Dr Livingstone,' he growled. Then he seemed to soften a little. His mouth twisted into a sneer. 'Oh, very well,' he said. He lifted a hand into the air. 'The softie is pardoned.'

There was a commotion from the crowd then, a mixture of anger and delight. It was clear that most statues belonged in the first camp, but it was just as obvious that they weren't about to go against the decision of their king. 'Now, be on your way,' cried Charlie. 'Go and see to the things you have to do and

I shall meet with you all again tonight at the Agon, where hopefully we will enjoy a good evening's entertainment.' He pointed to David. 'You and the Colonel shall remain behind,' he added. 'And we'll see what's to be done about the boy.'

Ed remembered to breathe. He sat there waiting as the crowd began to disperse, drifting off in various directions. As they trudged past, several statues threw grudging looks in Ed's direction. David wandered back to his companions and gave Ed a wink.

'That was close,' murmured the Colonel. 'For a moment there, I thought it was going to end badly.'

'You wouldn't have let them do it, would you?' asked Ed.

'I don't see how we'd have stopped them,' admitted David. 'We were somewhat outnumbered.'

'You pulled a brilliant trick there,' murmured the Colonel. 'But be warned, my friend, Charlie doesn't like people getting the better of him.'

The last of the statues left the square, but then two new ones appeared from the entrance of the building behind the plinth, two naked men carrying a long wooden plank between them.

'Who are *they*?' whispered Ed.

'Just a couple of Gormleys,' said David, mysteriously. 'They usually stand in the Waters of Leith.'

'Yes, but who are they meant to be?'

'That's an interesting question. The sculptor based them all on casts of his own body. He apparently is a brilliant fellow, but because he's still alive and because he's diluted his intelligence into so many different figures... there are six of them in Edinburgh and goodness knows how many across the country... well, I'm afraid they've each inherited only a tiny part of his genius.'

'Which means,' added the Colonel, 'that they're pleasant enough, if a little dim. They're good at doing what they're told, which means they are given all the menial tasks at the Calling. Charlie loves them because they follow his orders without asking questions.'

'They should put some clothes on,' murmured Ed.

'Indeed,' said the Colonel. 'It's very unsettling. But that's modern art for you. An excuse to shock all who look upon it.'

The Gormleys propped the plank against the side of the plinth, creating a steep gangway. The king dismounted from his horse and came down the plank, moving carefully. Ed noticed how the thick wood sagged in the middle under his weight. When Charlie was on firm ground, the horse followed and for a few moments the plank looked in real danger of snapping in two. 'Why doesn't he just get the horse to jump down?' asked Ed.

'You must be joking,' said the Colonel. 'Charlie and his horse are made of lead. If he tried that, they'd smash clean through the flagstones.'

Once the horse was safely down, Charlie handed the reins to one of the Gormleys and then strode closer to Ed and his companions. Ed could understand why the king felt so touchy about his appearance. He had a kind of leafy decoration perched on his head. He wore a short, girlish toga, what looked like a pair of leggings that ended at his shins and some flat sandals on his otherwise bare feet. He did look a bit of a twit, to be honest. Close up, Ed could see that he had a rather beaky nose and a round, glum face. He extended a hand and Ed shook it heartily, then realised by the Colonel's sharp intake of breath, that he'd done something wrong again.

'You're supposed to kiss it!' hissed the Colonel.

'Oh, er… sorry. Didn't realise.' Ed lifted the hand to his face and kissed the back of it. It had an unpleasant taste, which he supposed must be the lead. He made an effort not to grimace. 'Thanks, Charl… Your Majesty,' he stammered. 'For saving my life.'

'Don't flatter yourself,' said Charlie, his expression aloof. 'If just one of those idiots had volunteered, this would have ended differently and been far less trouble for me.' He looked at David. 'You're a slippery fellow, Dr Livingstone. Some might say too clever for your own good.'

David bowed his head. 'Your Majesty, ' he said. 'I was only trying to help.'

Charles sneered. 'I know exactly what you were doing,' he snapped. 'Your insolence has been noted.' He transferred his gaze to the Colonel. 'So,' he said, 'what do you propose to do with the boy?'

'Your Majesty?'

'Well, we can hardly let him wander about willy nilly, can we, getting under everyone's feet? We need to find out about him and once we know who he is, send him back to wherever he came from.'

'But I don't know how we'd do that,' said David. 'I mean, we're not detectives, are we?'

'I have enough to organise today without worrying about this,' said Charlie. He thought for a moment, tapping a sandaled foot on the flagstones and then he suddenly seemed to brighten up. 'Ah, Dr Livingstone, I declare that you have just given me a splendid idea.'

'I have?'

'Yes.' Charlie turned back to look up at the Colonel. 'A detective! Why don't you take him to our friend in Picardy Place?' he suggested. 'He's *always* claiming to have a talent at finding the answers to riddles.'

The Colonel frowned. 'Do you really think he can help?' he asked. 'There are many who say he's all talk and no substance.'

Charlie smiled. 'Well, this will be his opportunity to prove them wrong, won't it?' he said. 'Since he always refuses to join in the Agon or any of the other events we organise, it will be a test of his abilities.'

David seemed to be about to say something else, but the king held up a hand to silence him. 'That's it, I have made my decision,' he said. 'Colonel Alexander, you will see to this matter before you attend to anything else. And you shall impress upon our mutual friend that he has less than twenty-four hours to find a suitable solution. If he fails, I shall be far from impressed. Now, if you gentlemen will excuse me, I have more important matters to attend to.' With that, he turned away and strode towards the huge building beyond the plinth. The Gormleys fell into step behind him, one of them leading the king's horse by its reins. They all went in between the massive stone columns, out of sight.

The Colonel sighed. 'Well, that's that, I suppose,' he said. 'The king has spoken and we lesser beings can only obey.' He turned to look at David. 'I'll head on up to Picardy Place,' he said. 'I dare say I'll catch up with you later.'

David nodded. 'Yes, at the Agon, if not before.' He smiled up at Ed. 'I hope you find what you're looking for, lad. Good luck.' He reached out a hand to shake.

'Thanks,' said Ed. 'I'd say you just got me out of real trouble there.'

'Don't mention it.' David turned and strolled away across the square. 'I'm off to *Our Dynamic Earth*,' he shouted over his shoulder. 'I want to see what country they're focusing on this time. It's always entertaining but I'm still hoping that one year it'll be Africa.'

'Good luck,' said the Colonel. 'See you later!' He wheeled Sultan around and headed back to the road. Once there, he urged the horse into a brisk trot, then a canter and finally, a gallop. Ed clung on tightly to the Colonel's waist as they went along the road, Sultan's metal hooves throwing out a fearsome din.

'I don't understand!' shouted Ed. 'Who *is* this person we're going to see?'

But the Colonel either couldn't hear him over the noise of Sultan's hooves or wasn't prepared to give an answer. So Ed clung on for dear life, as they raced on through the darkness.

EIGHT

The Bronze Detective

They finally came to a place where a roundabout led to a small flagstoned square, fenced off behind a row of trees. The Colonel reined in Sultan and trotted in through the entrance, where there was an empty stone plinth.

'Damn the man,' muttered the Colonel, stating the obvious. 'He's not here.'

As he turned Sultan around, Ed caught a glimpse of a plaque on the side of the plinth and managed to catch the first few words of it. 'In memory of Sir Arthur Conan Doyle,' it read. The name meant nothing to him, but he supposed this must be the man they were looking for. He was going to ask the Colonel for more information, but he was already spurring Sultan on along the street, looking frantically to left and right as he did so and muttering a series of curses under his breath. Then, just a short distance onwards, he and Ed caught sight of the life-sized statue of a man kneeling in front of a huge, glass-fronted building on the far side of the road. The statue was examining something on the ground and he appeared to be deep in thought. He was wearing an odd-looking peaked hat with side flaps that were buttoned up on the top of his head. He wore a long overcoat and on top of that, a kind of short cloak tied at the neck and hanging to his waist. As soon as Ed laid eyes on him, he had a strong feeling of recognition. He knew this man from somewhere or at least, he recognised the distinctive outfit he was wearing. But the name he'd seen on the plaque didn't seem to fit.

The Colonel urged Sultan across the road and as they drew closer he shouted, 'Hey! Mr Holmes. May I have a word?'

That served to jog something in Ed's mind. He knew instantly what the man's first name was. Sherlock. And he also knew what he was famous for. It tied in with something that David had said earlier. Sherlock Holmes was a detective and, Ed thought, a rather famous one.

Sherlock looked up, his expression quizzical. Now Ed could see that, unlike most of the other statues he'd encountered, this one had a face that was clean-shaven. He held a distinctively shaped pipe in one hand. His intense gaze fell on Ed and his eyebrows raised ever so slightly, but unlike the others, he refrained from passing comment. 'Colonel Alexander,' he said, quietly, in a suave English voice. 'To what do I owe this unexpected pleasure?'

The Colonel reined Sultan to a halt. 'Charlie sent me to find you,' he said. 'As you can see, we have a bit of a problem on our hands.'

Sherlock nodded. 'I can't say I'm surprised,' he said, getting to his feet and slipping the pipe into the pocket of his overcoat. 'It was bound to happen sooner or later.' Now he was upright, Ed could see that he was a foot or so taller than life-sized. 'Who is the boy?' asked Sherlock.

'That's just the problem. The lad is suffering from amnesia. Charlie thought *you* might be just the man to find out who he is.'

Sherlock gave a thin smile.

'Did he now? My goodness, you mean to say, the king of Edinburgh actually acknowledged my existence?'

The Colonel sighed. 'Don't start,' he murmured.

'It seems to me that on other occasions, he has been rather critical.'

'That may be so, but…'

'Of course, I *do* specialise in mysteries,' added Sherlock. 'And it is my business to know what other people don't know.'

'Good. Then here's your chance to prove your mettle. I'm to leave the boy in your tender care.' The Colonel grabbed Ed unceremoniously around the waist, lifted him from the saddle and deposited him in front of the bronze detective. 'I need to be about my own business,' he said. 'I have a lot to do before tonight's Agon. Charlie says you have until then to work out who the boy is and where he's from.' He leaned forward in the saddle. 'He's under the king's protection, so nothing untoward is to happen to him. I trust I make myself clear.'

'Crystal, old boy.' Sherlock studied Ed for a moment, then turned back to the Colonel. 'And what if I don't wish to take the case?' he asked.

The Colonel grinned. 'I really don't think you have much choice. As you know, Charlie's word is law.'

Sherlock shrugged. 'There are some among us who would challenge his right to make such orders,' he said. 'Just because he's been around the longest, doesn't mean he automatically has the authority. There are some who would say that Victoria has every bit as much of a claim to the throne.'

The Colonel shook his head. 'I'm not going to sit here and debate politics with you,' he said. 'Let's just say that you'd be well advised to do as Charlie suggests. He was talking about executing people earlier.' He looked down at Ed and winked. 'I'll see you later,' he said. 'Now listen. Don't you take any nonsense from this fellow.'

And with that, he wheeled Sultan around and set off along the road at a brisk canter. Sherlock gazed calmly after him until he had gone a hundred yards or so. 'Military men,' he muttered. 'They're all basically the same. Reminds me so much of dear old Watson.'

Then finally he turned back to look down at Ed. 'Do you actually talk?' he asked.

'Course I do,' said Ed.

'And you really don't remember anything?'

'Well, not much. There's the odd thing I know but I don't know *how* I know, if you see what I mean?'

'Absolutely. And you have a name?'

'I suppose I must have, but I don't remember that either. The others have started calling me Ed.'

Sherlock rolled his eyes. 'Ed?' he muttered.

'Yeah, for Edinburgh.'

'Doesn't exactly show an awful lot of imagination,' said Sherlock. 'But following their logic, perhaps 'Manny' would have been more appropriate.'

Ed stared at him. 'What makes you say that?'

'Well, you're so evidently from Manchester, it would seem a logical choice.'

Ed stared at him. 'How do you know that?' he asked. 'We've only just met!'

'True, but I've heard you speak. Those vowel intonations could only have originated in darkest Manchester... though I'm not yet sure of the exact location. It will come to me.' Sherlock turned away and went back to where he'd been standing when the Colonel had ridden up. He indicated some marks on the ground. 'I was just examining the spot where my friends the *camelopardalis* usually dwell.'

'The... what?'

'The giraffes? It's always been my hope that one of

these years they'll hang around long enough for me to try to converse with them, but every year it's the same. The clock strikes twelve and off they go.'

'Oh, I saw *them*! Dreaming Spires? They were galloping along Princes Street like the clappers.'

'Hmm. There's a real mystery there. Since they race off in such a hurry, how is it they manage to eventually calm themselves and find their way home just in time for the changeover? Is it some kind of in-built homing system that guides them back to their site? That's something I intend to find out.'

Ed frowned. 'Look, I'm sorry, I'm a bit confused…'

'Well, of course you are, my boy. You're an amnesiac who's stumbled onto something that no softie… ridiculous name, and I absolutely refuse to use it… that no *human* should ever be a witness to.'

'Er… yeah, but I kind of *know* you. I think… are you… are you on the telly?'

Sherlock sighed. 'Yes, apparently I am. It's all anybody ever talks about when they come to look at me, these days. You know what I heard one moron saying to his friend? He doesn't look anything like Cumberbatch! Which is, of course, the name of the actor who portrays me. Honestly, when you hear remarks like that, you really do despair for the human race.'

'Umm… there's something I don't understand.'

'You surprise me. What is it, pray tell?'

'Well, on the thingy you stand on. The stone thing…'

'The plinth?'

'Yeah. It said you were called Sir Arthur something or other.'

'That's not *me*, you idiot. That's the name of my creator.'

'Your what?'

'The man who wrote me.'

'Oh, right, you mean for the telly?'

Sherlock took a deep breath. 'You're as bad as the rest of them,' he snarled. 'For your information, *Ed*, Sherlock Holmes was the hero of a series of stories long before they ever invented television. The author, Sir Arthur Conan Doyle, was born in Picardy Place. That's why they put my statue here.'

Ed struggled to make sense of this. 'Why... why didn't they make a statue of *him*?' he asked.

'Because I, his creation, became more famous than he ever was,' said Sherlock. 'Of course, it's always been a bone of contention with so many of the other statues.'

'Has it?'

'Oh yes. Ever since they put me here in 1991...'

'Oh, so you're a blow-in!'

Sherlock grimaced. 'I believe that's the term they use. Yes, because I'm not based on a real person, but a character from fiction, the general perception seems to be that I'm some kind of... imposter. I've tried telling them that the transference process is exactly the same, that I possess all the attributes of my famous progenitor, but they remain unconvinced.'

'Your famous *what*?'

'I have all of Sherlock Holmes' skills.'

'Oh, I see. Well, that thing about me being from Manchester was pretty clever. *If* you're right.'

'Of course I'm right. I'm *always* right. All one has to do is eliminate the impossible and what remains, however improbable…'

'Umm. Sorry, can I…?'

Sherlock rolled his eyes again. 'What is it?' he asked impatiently.

'It's just… I'm really hungry.'

'Hungry?' Sherlock scowled. 'When did you last…? Oh, of course, you don't know, do you?' He looked around for a moment. 'Hmm,' he murmured. 'We'll need to find you some food… but where? Where? Ah yes, follow me. We'll find something on Calton Road.' He started off along the road at a brisk walk and Ed followed him.

'Don't you ever eat?' he asked.

'Me? I'm a statue.'

'Yes, but I thought maybe, you know, this one night a year, you might be able to… eat a bag of crisps or something.'

'For goodness sake, boy, I have no digestive system, how would I ever manage to get food inside me?' He smiled. 'Mind you, having said that, I have witnessed statues trying to imbibe alcohol at the Agon. Not a pretty sight. It just dribbles down the front of them. I suppose it's a nostalgic thing. Robbie Burns and Robert

Louis Stevenson made a real exhibition of themselves last year. A waste of good malt whisky, if you ask me. But I appreciate it's different for humans. So of course, we'll find you some food.'

Just then, a small metal four-legged creature came scampering across the road towards them, wagging its stumpy tail.

'Oh my giddy aunt,' muttered Sherlock.

Ed saw that it was a little dog, some kind of a curly-haired terrier. It was made of black metal but for some reason it had a bright shiny golden nose. It was jumping up excitedly at Sherlock, but he was making a point of paying no attention to it. When it got no reaction from the detective it started on Ed, jumping up to place its front paws against his legs, but being made of metal, this was a dangerous thing to do and Ed was nearly knocked off his feet.

'Go home, Bobby!' snapped Sherlock. 'Isn't there a grave you should be lying on?'

'You know him?' asked Ed.

'Everyone in Edinburgh knows him,' said Sherlock. 'He's a pest. You've never heard of Greyfriar's Bobby?'

Ed shook his head. 'No, never.'

'Lucky you,' said Sherlock wistfully.

'What's up with his nose?'

'Tourists are rather fond of touching it for luck. Gives it a polished appearance.'

'He seems to like you.'

'Yes. I think he's drawn to me because we have something in common.'

'Oh, what's that?'

'Well, by all accounts he's pretty fictional too. I mean, he's sold to the tourists as part of Edinburgh's history, but when you examine the records, the evidence for his existence is somewhat sketchy. Calm down, Bobby! Down!'

Bobby seemed to get the message and stopped jumping up, but he trotted happily along behind the two of them as they walked. Sherlock continued to talk.

'He was supposed to have belonged to a night watchman at Greyfriar's Kirkyard. When the man died, so the story goes, Bobby here was alleged to have lain on the man's grave for fourteen years.' Sherlock raised his eyebrows. 'Bearing in mind that every dog year is worth seven of a human's life, and the fact that he must have been around for a few years *before* his owner died, that would make him well over a hundred years old when he finally trotted off to doggie heaven. Quite an unlikely age for a Skye Terrier, I think you'll agree. The only possible explanation is that there must have been more than one dog. He was replaced several times in order to keep the story going.'

'Why would they do that?' asked Ed.

'Because, dear boy, he's one of Edinburgh's top tourist attractions and has been for many years.' Sherlock rubbed a thumb and forefinger together.

'Money is a powerful motivator in these cases,' he said. 'I believe the story has some basis in fact, but it's been somewhat exaggerated over the years.' He looked up as an illuminated sign came into view. 'Ah, this is the place I was looking for.'

Ed gazed up at it. 'Starbucks?' he muttered.

'I'm sure we'll find something edible in here,' said Sherlock. He stepped up to the plate glass doors, reached into his pocket and took out a small bunch of metal picks. He inserted one of them into the lock and fiddled around for a few moments, twisting it this way and that. There was a sharp click and he was able to push the doors open. Immediately an alarm went off, a shrill clanging sound, but Sherlock stepped up to a metal box on the wall and started tapping the keys on the side of it, his hand moving through a sequence of numbers at lightning fast speed, his metal index finger a blur. 'There are only so many possible combinations,' he explained calmly, 'but I'm going to run through the most likely ones first.'

'Will somebody come?' asked Ed nervously.

'Oh no, nobody's interested tonight. But we want to hear ourselves think, don't we?' After a few moments, the alarm stopped suddenly and Sherlock looked vaguely disappointed. 'The month and the year,' he said disparagingly. 'You'd have thought they'd have tried to make it a tad more difficult than that.'

He turned back to smile at Ed and gestured towards

the glass counter, which Ed could see was liberally heaped with sandwiches, cakes and biscuits.

'Help yourself,' suggested Sherlock.

'I need to pop somewhere first,' Ed told him, nodding meaningfully towards the sign that read 'Toilets.' 'You know, pay a visit and all that.'

'Ah yes, of course,' said Sherlock. 'Another little problem we statues don't have. You run along.'

'Thanks.' Ed headed gratefully for the conveniences and Sherlock called after him.

'Why don't I pick out a selection of food for you? And then, while you dine, the two of us shall have a little talk.'

NINE

Looking For Clues

Ed returned from the toilets to find Sherlock sitting at a table with a whole assortment of food piled on top of it. There was everything from sandwiches and crisps to cake and flapjack, all sealed in cellophane packages.

'I'll never eat all this,' protested Ed, settling into the seat opposite.

'Take whatever you fancy,' said Sherlock. 'I wasn't sure what you liked, so I picked out a variety.'

'I haven't got the money to pay for it,' Ed warned him.

Sherlock waved a bronze hand as though it was of no consequence. 'This lot was almost certainly destined for the bins,' he said. 'They'll be restocking first thing tomorrow morning.' He leaned closer. 'Besides, from what I've heard, this company is only one of many who play fast and loose with their tax returns. I'm sure a few free sandwiches aren't going to sink them.'

Ed frowned. He searched through the selection of sandwiches and picked out a cheese and chutney one. He was pretty sure that was something he liked. He didn't know *how* he knew this and yet, when he bit into it, he enjoyed the flavour. He popped the ring pull on a can of lemonade. On the floor beside him, Bobby looked up hopefully, his stumpy tail wagging. 'He looks like he wants something,' Ed observed.

'Force of habit,' Sherlock assured him. 'He couldn't swallow food if he tried.' He leaned back in his chair, which creaked alarmingly beneath his heavy frame. It clearly wasn't designed to take the weight of a bronze statue. 'Right,' said Sherlock. 'Let's begin, shall we? Tell me, what can you remember?'

Ed chewed thoughtfully on a mouthful of sandwich.

'Not very much,' he said. 'I mean, I *know* stuff… like, for instance, I knew who you were, pretty much as soon as I saw you. Because of the weird hat.'

'It's called a deerstalker. Never mentioned in any of the stories, of course. In *The Adventure of Silver Blaze*, Sir Arthur did describe me as wearing an ear-flapped travelling cap, but the deerstalker of course, was popularised in the Basil Rathbone films of the nineteen forties.'

'Er… right.' Ed hesitated for a moment, his thoughts interrupted. 'And then, when I was talking to Sir William Scott…'

'Sir *Walter* Scott.'

'Yes, him! I realised that I knew the name of another author and the books *she* wrote. So, stuff like that... things I must have known from before.'

Sherlock nodded. 'Anything else?' he asked.

'Well, there was this other weird thing that happened. Sir Walter was telling me the names of some of his books...'

'Yes?'

'... and he said there was one called *The Peveril of the Peak*. And that meant something to me.'

'Perhaps you've read it?'

Ed shook his head. 'I don't think so. It sounded a bit... you know, old fashioned? Not really my sort of thing. At least, I don't *think* it is. But then I saw something, kind of like in my head.'

'A vision?'

'I suppose. It was this old building and it was like all covered in green tiles? And it had those same words written over the door.'

'*The Peveril of the Peak*?'

'Yes. And then I saw this man, going in through the door.'

'Good.' Sherlock seemed pleased by this. 'What next?'

'That's all really. The door swung shut.'

'Did you recognise him?'

'No. He was turned away from me. I didn't see his face. He just looked... like an ordinary guy, you know?'

'How was he dressed?'

'What do you mean?'

'Well, was he smart or scruffy? Did he wear modern clothing or…?'

Ed thought for a moment, trying to picture the scene. 'He was wearing… a black leather jacket, I think… and blue jeans.'

'Shoes?'

'Trainers, maybe.' Ed closed his eyes for a moment. 'Yeah. White trainers.'

'What about his hair?'

'Umm… longish, I think. You know, over his collar.'

'Well, that's something,' said Sherlock. 'You see, often people believe they haven't noticed anything but when you prompt them, it's surprising how much detail they actually took in.' He leaned closer. 'You know, the world is full of obvious things that, by chance, nobody ever observes.'

'Umm… right.' Ed was about to ask a question but he felt something nudging against his leg and looking down, he saw that Bobby was pawing at him, still with that pleading expression on his face.

'Oh, my giddy aunt,' muttered Sherlock. 'Give him a biscuit. He'll soon realise he can't do anything with it.'

Ed searched through the pile of food until he located a packet of shortbreads. He ripped open the cellophane and handed Bobby a biscuit, which he managed to take into his mouth. He then spent some time trying to swallow it without success, twisting his head this way and that and making a series of pitiful whimpering sounds, before dropping the pieces on to the floor and poking at them miserably with one paw.

'Ignore him,' suggested Sherlock. 'He's just looking for attention. So, tell me, what else can you remember?'

Ed shrugged. 'That's about it. Oh, yeah, I knew who David Livingstone was. I felt like maybe I'd learned about him at school.'

'Hmm. Seems likely enough. But you've no idea *which* school?'

'No. Sorry.' Ed took another bite of his sandwich. 'Bit rubbish, isn't it?'

Sherlock didn't say anything. He leaned forward over the table and started ruffling Ed's hair with two huge fingers.

'What are you doing?' Ed asked him.

'Looking for a bump… cuts, abrasions, that sort of thing. You're not aware of any soreness of the head, any aches or pains?'

'Well, now you mention it…'

'You see, there are two types of amnesia,' continued Sherlock, still examining Ed's scalp. 'There's the retrograde kind, which typically is the inability to remember incidents before a specific date, perhaps when you had an accident of some kind. Then there's anterograde, which is defined as an inability to transfer new information from the short-term memory store to the long-term.'

Ed took a gulp of his lemonade. 'I'll… take your word for it,' he said. 'But what sort do you…?'

'Ah hah!' said Sherlock.

'Ah hah what?'

'There's definitely signs of a contusion here on the side of your head. You've had a bump and not so very long ago. Is that sore at all?' Sherlock prodded Ed's skull with a huge index finger and he gave a grunt of pain.

'It is a bit,' he said.

Sherlock leaned back in his seat, which gave another ominous creak. 'I would conjecture that this is more than just a coincidence. I think you've recently had some kind of an accident that has made you lose your memory.'

Ed frowned. 'Can that happen?' he asked.

'It's not unheard of. I believe you're suffering from what doctors would call dissociative amnesia. And it might be more than just the accident that's caused it. It could be that it happened when you were undergoing something that was profoundly upsetting, so terrible that your brain has chosen to make you forget all about it. Perhaps the image of the man going through the door is a clue. Perhaps your unconscious mind is trying to help you remember something that happened in the recent past.' He frowned, tapped his bronze fingers loudly on the table top for a while. 'Very well,' he said. 'Now turn out your pockets.'

'Eh?'

'You heard me. I want to see everything you have in them. Put it all out on the table.'

Ed frowned, remembering how he'd done all that at the train station when he was looking for a ticket, but he did as he was told, reaching into each pocket in turn and taking out whatever he found there. He set the items down, one by one. It was a sorry-looking collection. A handful of loose change; a sheet of folded paper; a small bundle of cards secured with an elastic band; another smaller scrap of paper, and a single metal key.

'That's it?' asked Sherlock, incredulously.

'I'm afraid so. It isn't much to go on, is it?'

Sherlock didn't say anything. He picked up the coins first and went through them in detail. 'So, what have we here? A Scottish one pound coin featuring the thistle and bluebell, and a Northern Irish one featuring a shamrock and flax, both dated 2014.' He frowned, turned each of them over and then set them down, before continuing. 'A Commonwealth Games fifty pence piece also dated 2014. A twenty pence piece featuring the English Rose and dated 2000. A ten pence piece featuring two rampant lions, dated 2014. A two pence piece featuring the classic three feathers design dated 1972. And a one pence piece featuring a portcullis, dated 2007.'

Ed looked at him. 'What does all that tell us?' he asked.

'Only one thing,' said Sherlock. 'That you're not

exactly a millionaire. Do you not have any paper money on your person?'

Ed shook his head. 'I couldn't find any,' he said.

'You see, that doesn't make any sense,' said Sherlock. 'Who would allow a boy of around thirteen years of age to travel from Manchester to Edinburgh, a journey of more than two hundred miles, without issuing him with some means of buying food and drink?'

'We don't really know that I've *come* from Manchester,' Ed reminded him.

'Of course we do,' Sherlock assured him. 'The more I hear you speak, the more convinced I am. In fact, I would now be willing to narrow the field down more and say that you're almost certainly from *South* Manchester.'

'What makes you say that?'

'It's in the way you say certain words,' said Sherlock. 'Only a native of that area would roll his vowels in that peculiar manner. I'd bet money on it. Tell me, boy, on the train... did you not have any baggage with you? A suitcase, a duffel?'

'No. I had a quick look after everyone else had got off but there was no luggage left. I don't think anyone stole my bags or anything.'

'In that case, I deduce that you came away from Manchester suddenly, without making any plans to do so. Your trip was unplanned... perhaps even accidental. It could just be.... that you were trying to escape from somebody.'

Now Sherlock picked up the pack of cards. He removed the elastic bands and fanned them out on the table. This time, Ed saw something that *he* recognised.

'Top Trumps!' he said.

'The Dinosaur Edition,' added Sherlock. 'You're a follower of the game?'

Ed shrugged. 'Maybe,' he said. 'I mean, I know how it works, but… I don't really remember playing it myself.'

'Why else would you carry them with you? Not a full pack here, mind you. Just some spares, as though you might be looking to swap them.' He pointed. 'See, you have two Triceratops here and three Pachycephalosaurus.'

'Hmm.' Ed looked at Sherlock. 'I'm amazed you even know about Top Trumps. It's a pretty modern game, isn't it?'

'Oh, not as modern as you might suspect! The cards were originally issued in 1977, by a company named Dubreq. They were taken over by Waddingtons in 1982, who continued producing them until the early 1990s. In 1999, of course, the rights were purchased by a company called Winning Moves. They decided to relaunch them, offering a range of more diverse topics. These particular cards though, belong to their *Classics* series. They came out in the year 2000 and are really quite collectible.'

Once again, Ed found himself staring at the bronze detective.

'How could you know all that?' he cried. 'It must be way after your time.'

Sherlock looked a little sheepish. 'Well, of course, I still continue to study. I… I use the internet to read up on new developments. It's a bit of a passion, actually. I spend hours at a time on it.'

'But… how? You only have one day a year!'

'Er… no, not strictly true. I er…' Sherlock sighed. 'I didn't really want to tell you about this, but the fact is, I cheat.' He reached up a hand and removed his deerstalker hat, revealing a flat metal box fixed to the top of his head, on which some little red lights flashed rhythmically.

'What is *that*?' cried Ed.

Sherlock, looking rather guilty. 'It's… er, well, actually, it's a modem.'

TEN

New-Fangled

'You see,' continued Sherlock, 'since my birth as a statue in 1991, I was so *bored* standing around for three hundred and sixty four days of the year. I wanted to learn more but I had no way of doing it. So, at my very first Calling, once I'd adjusted to the wonder of it all, I resolved to rectify the situation. I spent the entire twenty-four hours building the first version of this.' He pointed to the device on his head. 'Over the years I've developed it more and more. That's why the other statues accuse me of being standoffish, you see. While they are at the Agon, reading their silly poems and so forth, I'm generally at the University of Edinburgh, putting the finishing touches to my latest modifications.' He tapped the box on his head. 'This is just a modem.' He took his pipe from his pocket. 'And this is my mouse. Since I am required to hold it the whole time I'm on the plinth, no human ever notices if I tap the stem occasionally.'

'I didn't think you could move on normal days!'

Sherlock looked guilty. 'Officially I can't and it's forbidden to try anyway, so *please* don't mention it to the others!' He replaced his hat. 'But over the years, after much mental cogitation and experimentation, I have managed to obtain the permanent use of my right index finger.'

Ed stared at him in amazement. 'What do you do for electricity?' he asked.

'Oh, well, the earlier version utilised batteries, but they always ran out after a few weeks, leaving me bored to tears. *Now* the system is solar-powered. I tell you what, if the people at Apple ever found out about this, they'd be after it like a shot!' He looked thoughtful for a moment. 'Absolutely the worst time for me was when I was removed from Picardy Place in order for the tramline to be built. I spent three years in a warehouse, wrapped up in canvas. Obviously the modem's battery ran out after a few days and I was unable to recharge it. I can't begin to tell you how bored I was that first year!'

'Must have been awful,' murmured Ed.

'Well, luckily, when the next Calling came around, I was able to get free of the wrapping and I managed to get over to the University where I put together a little device which I attached to a skylight in the warehouse. This enabled me to recharge the modem on a daily basis, despite having to remain covered up. So the next two years were somewhat easier. At least I was able to study! When they finally brought me back out into the daylight, I swear I could have cried.'

'So... how does it work exactly?' asked Ed. 'The modem. I mean, you're standing on a plinth all day so...'

Sherlock smiled proudly. 'I wasn't going to let you see this, but I suppose the cat's out of the bag now, so why don't I give you a little demonstration? Watch this.' He pressed something on the pipe and a curved glass screen descended smoothly from the brim of his hat, in front of his eyes. 'I stole this idea from Google Glass,' he whispered. 'The words are projected invisibly onto the screen. Of course, I have to be very careful when I use it. Late at night, obviously, when there are no humans around. I've spent many happy hours browsing my way through Wikipedia, just reading up on whatever interests me. Now, what were we talking about earlier? Oh yes, *The Peveril of the Peak*.' He tapped his pipe a few times, his bronze fingers moving rhythmically and Ed saw his gaze intensify as he stared at something on the curved screen that only he could see. 'Ah! It appears that as well as the novel, there's a hotel in Ashbourne with that name and... yes! As I suspected! A public house in the city of Manchester.' He tapped the pipe again. 'Let's see some images... hmm! It's a very distinctive building. Victorian, obviously. Completely covered in green tiles.'

'That's what I saw!' said Ed excitedly. 'And the sign's above the door?'

'Yes, yes, just as you described it. Which also confirms my suspicions about your home.' Sherlock tapped the pipe and the screen slid silently back into the brim. He dropped the pipe back into his pocket. 'Now, where was I? Oh, yes…'

He returned his attention to the cards. 'I really don't think these will be much help to us,' he said. 'All they tell me is that you play Top Trumps and that you very likely trade cards with other players. It would also suggest that you have a working knowledge of dinosaurs. Let me try something.' He gazed thoughtfully at Ed. 'World's biggest dinosaur?' he murmured.

'Argentinosaurus,' said Ed, without thinking. 'It used to be Apatosaurus, but they just discovered this new one in…'

'…Argentina,' finished Sherlock. 'Yes, well I suppose that answers the question fairly neatly.' He set the cards down and picked up the key.

'A Chubb key,' he observed. 'A fairly ordinary thing. I'm guessing that it's probably the key to the door of your home in Manchester. Now, what's interesting about it is that it's not a Yale.'

'What does that mean?' asked Ed.

'A Chubb lock is of a better quality than a Yale, because it uses a lever tumbler system that can only be operated by a mortice key, like this one. Now, you'll note that this is a copy…'

'How can you tell?'

Sherlock held the key out so Ed could see it better. He indicated a couple of initials stamped into the head of it. 'Some locksmiths, whenever they copy a key, stamp a mark of recognition onto it, in order to identify it as their work. You see, it says J. S, which is likely to be a name, John Smith or whatever. Some locksmiths even go so far as to include a phone number for their premises, but alas, not in this case. That would have made things a whole lot easier. Who knows? It might have been a local establishment, just around the corner from where you actually live.'

'Wow,' murmured Ed. 'That would have been handy.'

'Wouldn't it just? But I have learned that in these matters things do not always go to plan.' He paused for a moment as though something had just caught his attention. 'We've missed something,' he said.

'Have we? What's that?'

Sherlock pointed a huge index finger at Ed's chest. 'There's a slight bulge,' he said. 'It looks to me as though you have something hidden under your clothing.'

'Really?'

'Yes. Have a look. It's clearly something you always carry, which would explain why you were not aware of it.'

Ed slid a hand under his t-shirt and realised that the detective was right. After a bit of fishing around, he found that there was something hanging around his neck on a length of twine. He pulled it out and held it up so that Sherlock could see it.

It was a chunky metal whistle. Sherlock took it from him and blew experimentally down it, producing nothing but a faint hissing sound. Oddly, Bobby lifted his metal ears and began to wag his tail frantically. 'It would seem you're a dog owner,' announced Sherlock.

'What makes you say that?'

'The whistle makes a sound that is only audible to the canine and feline ear.' He indicated Bobby who was still looking intently up at them.

'Then maybe I'm a cat owner,' suggested Ed.

Sherlock smiled. 'Unlikely. Nobody in their right mind would attempt to train a cat! Of course, we know you're *not* in your right mind, but we must at least assume that you were before you lost your memory.' He seemed to concentrate for a moment. 'The dog whistle was invented by Francis Galton in 1876 for the express purpose of training dogs. Why else would you carry one with you?'

Ed took the whistle from Sherlock and looked at it with interest, but it meant nothing to him. He tried blowing into it, an act that only stirred Bobby up again.

'That also explains the business of the hairs,' muttered Sherlock. 'Which is good, because it was puzzling me.'

'Hairs?' muttered Ed.

'Yes.' Sherlock reached into a pocket and pulled out a pair of metal tweezers. He leaned across the table and plucked something from the sleeve of Ed's coat – a single black hair. He drew back his arm and examined the hair closely. 'I noticed earlier that you have several of these stuck to your jacket. They're clearly not yours… and judging by the coarse nature of them, they're not of human origin, either. It's hard to say conclusively without the use of a microscope, but I would guess at a longhaired variety of dog, black in colour with… occasional white markings. I'm no great expert on canines but I'd suggest this is a hair from a border collie.'

Ed was vaguely aware of his jaw dropping open. 'You can tell all that just by looking at it?' he cried.

'Simple deduction,' said Sherlock, with surprising modesty. He dropped the hair on the table, replaced the tweezers and went to hand the whistle back to Ed. He weighed it in his hand for a moment. 'It's extremely heavy for its size,' he muttered. 'Here, hang it around your neck again, while I look at the other things.' He picked up the small scrap of paper and unfolded it. There were six digits written on it in biro. 1-6-0-7-0-2.

'What do you suppose that means?' muttered Ed.

'It's some kind of code,' said Sherlock. 'I would guess at a combination, perhaps for a lock, an alarm or a safe, something of that kind. The digits suggest to me that it could be somebody's birthday… possibly yours. The sixteenth of July, 2002? Does that ring any bells?'

Ed shook his head. 'Nothing rings any bells,' he muttered.

'Well, I'd judge you to be around thirteen years of age,' said Sherlock. 'So a birth year of 2002 seems quite likely to me. Anyway, we'll set this aside for now. Which leaves us with just one more thing and I have kept what I think could be the most interesting item until last.' He picked up the bigger square of paper and unfolded it, something that Ed hadn't even thought to do when he'd first found it. Sherlock studied it for a moment in silence. 'How very strange,' he said, at last.

'What is it?' asked Ed.

'Have a look,' suggested Sherlock and handed him the sheet of paper.

Ed took it from him and studied it in silence for a moment. It was an A4 handbill, what looked like a homemade affair, printed off from a computer. There was a large picture of a black and white dog and at the bottom of the page in bold black letters was some information.

MISSING!
'Lucky.'
If you find him please phone

Annoyingly, the flyer had been roughly torn along the bottom edge and though it was possible to discern a row of smudges that must once have been the very tops of the eleven digits of a phone number, it was impossible to tell what they actually were.

'Weird,' said Ed. 'A dog.'

'Not just any dog,' said Sherlock, with a triumphant smile. He tapped the photograph with an index finger. 'Unless I'm very much mistaken, that is a border collie.'

ELEVEN

Lucky

Ed stared across the table at Sherlock. 'So… you reckon I've got a dog?'

'No,' Sherlock corrected. 'I think you *had* a dog. And I think you lost it.' He tapped the homemade poster. 'I'm guessing that you made this poster yourself. You probably printed several copies and stuck them up around your neighbourhood. I believe that's what people do in these circumstances.' He studied the poster for a moment. 'Furthermore, I don't think you had the dog for very long, before you lost it.'

'What makes you say that?'

Sherlock tapped the photograph again. 'Because "Lucky" can't be more than a year or so old,' he said.

'Oh, come on,' cried Ed. 'How can you tell that just by looking?'

'This is my method,' said Sherlock, calmly. 'It is founded upon the observation of trifles. I would direct your attention to two things.' He pointed to the dog's open mouth and lolling tongue. 'Look at those teeth,' he said. 'They're not milk teeth but adult ones, which a dog acquires from the age of about three and a half months. But also note that they are bright white with no sign whatsoever of any tartar build up, something that will inevitably occur when a dog is over a year old, no matter how much care the owner provides.' He moved the tip of his finger higher. 'Now consider the eyes. See how clear and bright they are? A dog's eyes tend to appear slightly duller past the age of two or three years. Assuming you had Lucky as a pup, that means you can't have been his owner for much more than ten months to a year… eighteen months at the very outside.'

Ed shook his head in admiration. 'You're amazing,' he said and Sherlock allowed himself a brief smile.

'I have my moments,' he admitted. He studied Ed. 'You have no recollection of making these posters?' he asked. 'There's no sense of familiarity about them?'

'No. Sorry.'

Sherlock frowned. 'The curious incident of the dog in the poster,' he murmured.

'Beg pardon?'

'Never mind. Just musing aloud.'

Ed shrugged, and looked down at the bronze dog sitting beside him. 'Perhaps we should show it to Bobby,' he suggested. 'See if he's got any ideas.'

Sherlock scowled. 'We're not *that* desperate,' he said. He waved a hand at the items on the table. 'We need a fresh perspective on this. I'm afraid Starbucks isn't suitably conducive to my thought processes. Collect up all these bits and pieces and replace them in your pockets. And help yourself to more of this food also. We don't want to have to keep stopping so you can feed your face.'

Ed did as he was told, selecting a couple of sandwiches, some biscuits and another can of lemonade. By the time he was finished, his pockets were bulging with supplies. Sherlock stood up from the table and his chair gave a final creak of relief but Ed noticed that the metal legs now looked permanently bowed. Ed stood up too.

'Where are we going?' he asked.

'Outside,' said Sherlock, 'where it's easier to think.' He led the way back to the main doors and Ed followed, with Bobby trotting along behind them. Sherlock swung open the glass door and indicated that Ed should step out onto the pavement. The detective paused to reset the alarm and as he stepped out, he began to swing the glass door back, trapping Bobby inside.

'Wait!' cried Ed. 'We can't leave him in here.'

Sherlock sighed. 'I suppose not,' he agreed. 'It's tempting, though. Just think of the furore *that* would cause. Greyfriars Bobby found sitting in a branch of Starbucks! That's a mystery they'd *never* solve.' He swung the door open again and waited while the little dog stepped daintily over the threshold. Then he swung it back, took out his picks and locked it.

He stood for a moment, as though deep in thought. The dawn was breaking on the horizon, a pale light coming up from behind the tall tenements to their left. Sherlock reached into his waistcoat pocket and pulled out an old fashioned fob watch. 'Four sixteen AM,' he muttered. 'Time is ticking away. I feel we need to try something more radical.' He seemed to come to a decision. 'Follow me,' he said and led the way back along Leith Walk. Ed fell in beside him and Bobby, his bronze tail still wagging, trotted happily along in their wake.

'Where are we going?' asked Ed.

'Just down the road a short distance,' said Sherlock. 'I need to obtain official permission.'

'Permission for what?' murmured Ed.

'Permission to try something unconventional.'

'You…. don't have a Dr Watson, do you?'

'No. Not that he ever gave me much help. Only when I was in a tight corner and I needed somebody handy with his fists. No, I'm going to…' He broke off suddenly as he noticed a figure in the distance coming towards them. 'Oh, my giddy aunt,' he muttered. He grabbed Ed's arm and pulled him towards a nearby shop doorway. Bobby stood there looking at them, puzzled. 'Heel!' snapped Sherlock and Bobby went obediently to him. 'Grab hold of that dog,' said Sherlock urgently. 'Make sure he doesn't bark or do anything to give us away.'

Ed took hold of Bobby, marvelling at the way his bronze body felt warm and malleable to the touch. He tried at first to pick him up, but quickly realised he was far too heavy for that, so instead he pulled him in close to his feet. 'Who's coming?' he whispered, but Sherlock just pressed himself into the shadow of the doorway and reached out a hand to pull Ed in beside him. The expression on the great detective's face was decidedly grim, Ed thought. They waited.

Now Ed could hear that whoever was coming along the street was singing heartily to himself in a broad Scottish accent.

'I have brought ye to the ring
Now dance if ye can!
I have brought ye to the revel
Now see if ye can dance!'

He kept singing the same lines over and over and this was accompanied by a rattling, clanking rhythm, as though somebody was shaking a bag of pots and pans. As the figure moved into sight, gazing straight ahead, Ed could see that the tall statue was fully encased in a suit of armour and was carrying a pointed shield and a huge broadsword. There was just a glimpse of a hawkish, moustachioed face glaring out from a strange piece of chain mail headgear. Ed thought the man was going to stride on past but he was still in plain view when he suddenly stopped singing and came to a halt, still gazing straight ahead.

'Don't think I didn't see you,' he growled, in a low, rumbling voice that sounded decidedly aggressive.

Ed glanced up at Sherlock in alarm, but the detective's face remained expressionless. There was a long silence.

'Well? Are ye going to skulk there in your doorway or are you going to step out here and face me like a man?'

Again, Sherlock gave no reply and made no attempt to move.

'It seems the others I have spoken to were correct in their observations,' snarled the statue. 'You really are all talk, aren't you? Somebody without the courage to back up his convictions.' Again, Sherlock made no reply and after a few moments, the stranger gave a derisive snort. 'Suit yourself. You can't hide from me forever, *Sassenach*. One day, you and I will meet face to face and then we'll see if *you* can dance.' And with that the stranger continued walking, his armoured feet clanking on the pavement. After he had gone a short distance he began to sing again, those same lines, repeated over and over.

> *'I have brought ye to the ring*
> *Now see if ye can dance...'*

Ed let out a sigh of relief but he noticed that Sherlock made no attempt to move until he was sure the other statue was well gone. Finally, he took his hand off Ed's shoulder and stepped cautiously out from the doorway.

He threw a wary glance up the road before continuing to walk. Ed fell into step beside him again, expecting him to say something by way of explanation, but Sherlock was strolling along, a scowl on his face, as though he was pondering something completely different. In the end, Ed had to prompt him.

'Who was that?' he asked.

'Hmm?' Sherlock looked down at him in surprise.

'Who was that who just spoke to us?'

'Oh, him.' Sherlock shrugged his shoulders. 'That was just Mad Willy.'

'Who?'

'That's what everyone calls him, around Edinburgh. William Wallace is his full name. Goodness knows what he was doing out here, he usually stays up around the castle.'

The name seemed to ring yet another bell with Ed. He thought that it might be something he'd learned in school.

'Why was he so nasty to you?'

'Because I'm English. He's not very fond of the English.'

'Oh, why not?'

Sherlock gave a thin smile. 'It's hard to say exactly. It could be because we murdered his wife and child... that would definitely have irked him. Or...'

'Or what?'

'It could be because we had him half strangled, then eviscerated...'

'E-what?'

'We pulled his insides out,' added Sherlock. 'While he was still alive. Then we burnt the guts in front of him, beheaded him and stuck his head up on a spike at the Gates of London. Let's face it, that's not going to endear you to anybody.'

Ed pulled a face. 'Eww! Why did we do all that to him?'

'He was a Scottish rebel leader,' explained Sherlock. 'This was back in the 1200s when Scotland was still under English rule. He won a few big battles to start with but... well, in the end, he lost and had to go on the run. Eventually, they caught him, put him on trial and... executed him in the most barbaric fashion. He's never really got over it. Now, he goes around looking for excuses to start trouble with anyone he doesn't feel is properly Scottish. Like me and you.' He shook his head. 'Like half the people in Edinburgh, to be honest.'

Ed frowned. 'Is there... was there some kind of film about him? Only, I'm getting this picture in my head of a man with a blue face...'

'Oh, never mention *that* to him!' said Sherlock. 'One year, his only friend, Robert the Bruce, took him to see that, thinking it might cheer him up. It just happened to be on at one of the cinemas on the night of the Calling. I'm afraid he was not impressed. Apparently it wasn't very accurate. And also, the actor who played him was...'

'What?' asked Ed.

'An Australian,' murmured Sherlock as though it was something shameful. 'You can imagine how delighted he was by that!'

'I've got a feeling I might have seen that film,' murmured Ed. 'Maybe on TV? Was there… was there a man with a blue face?'

'I really wouldn't know,' said Sherlock. 'I tend to avoid that kind of thing.'

'But there are films about you, aren't there? And TV programmes. Surely you must be interested to see how they've… done you?'

Sherlock made a face. 'I shudder to think *what* they've done,' he said. 'Of course, I've read about the various incarnations of me over the years, but I draw the line at actually watching the films. You know, somebody I spoke to told me about a series where I'm played by an American, and I go around fighting all the time! I mean, I'm not opposed to a bit of boxing but this fellow is a master of oriental martial arts or some such nonsense. If I knew how to do that, perhaps I would have stepped out of that doorway and taken on Mad Willy.'

'He *did* have a great big sword,' Ed reminded him.

'Yes, and I wouldn't doubt for a moment that he'd use it, if he felt like it.' Sherlock shook his head. 'He's bad enough on his own but when he and Robbie Bruce get together, the two of them are unbearable. It's just lucky they're not able to drink alcohol, otherwise who knows what might happen?'

Sherlock came to a halt and gazed across the road. 'Ah, good, she hasn't gone very far,' he murmured. Ed followed his gaze. He could see that they had come to a sort of junction and across the way there was a large wedge-shaped plaza in front of a shopping precinct. To the left of the flagged area, a tall metal spike was sticking up from the pavement with the words *New Kirkgate* emblazoned on them. To the right there was a large stone plinth, surrounded by railings. This was empty, but the bronze statue of a horse was tied to the railings by its reins. Off to one side of the plinth, a large wooden table had been set out on the stone flags and two bronze statues were seated at it, side-by-side. Around them, a series of much smaller statues were moving to and fro, carrying trays of what looked like food and drink, as though waiting on them.

'Come along,' said Sherlock and he began to lead the way across the road, but he paused when he noticed that Bobby was following them. 'Stay here,' he said, pointing to the pavement and Bobby dropped obediently into a sitting position, his ears down, a pleading expression on his face. 'Stay,' Sherlock repeated, just to be sure there was no mistake. Then he led the way across the road. As they drew nearer, Ed could see that one of the seated statues was a woman, and it occurred to him that this was surely the *only* female statue he'd seen since he'd arrived in Edinburgh. Beside her sat the statue of a man. He had pleasant features, with a neatly trimmed moustache and long sideburns that came right down to his jawline but Ed couldn't help noticing that he was a strange shade of pale green from head to foot. As Ed drew closer still, he saw that the woman was wearing a crown. The man was talking and she was listening to him intently, an enraptured smile on her face.

As Sherlock and Ed reached the far pavement, one of the other statues turned away from the table and hurried over to intercept them. Ed saw instantly that it was a Gormley, but this one looked somewhat different to the two that Ed had seen in Parliament Square. He was wearing a pair of red boxer shorts and an ill-fitting blue hoodie advertising the Edinburgh Fringe – whatever that was. The Gormley held up a hand and said, in a strange nasal voice. "Ow do? Kindly state yer business 'ere!' It was, Ed thought, a Yorkshire accent.

Sherlock smiled. 'Please tell Her Majesty that Mr Holmes is asking for permission to speak to her,' he said.

'Mr 'oo?'

Sherlock smiled politely. 'Sherlock Holmes... the famous detective?'

The Gormley grunted. He didn't have much in the way of features, just a series of bumps and angles where a face ought to be so it was hard to tell how he felt about the situation, but he turned obediently away and trotted off towards the table.

'Why's he wearing underpants?' whispered Ed.

Sherlock looked down at him. 'It's simply for the

sake of decency,' he said. 'Well, he can hardly walk around stark naked in front of Queen Victoria, can he?'

TWELVE

By Royal Appointment

Ed stared at the seated statue. '*That's* Queen Victoria?' he said. 'I didn't... I didn't think she looked like that!' He wasn't sure what had made him say this. For some reason the mention of her name had made him picture a little old lady with white hair. But this woman looked to be in her twenties or thirties.

'You're probably used to seeing her older,' murmured Sherlock. 'Most of her surviving photographs were taken much later on, when she was a widow. That statue depicts her as she was in 1842, when she first visited Scotland.'

'I see. So... does that mean...?'

'What?'

'Well, does she only know stuff that Victoria knew up to 1842... or does she know stuff from later on as well?'

'The statue was made *after* her death,' said Sherlock. 'So of course, she knows everything that Victoria knew in her entire lifetime.' He gave Ed a withering look. 'Try and keep up,' he said.

Ed studied what was going on at the table. Several smaller bronze statues were carrying trays of food and drink backwards and forwards between the big table and a smaller one standing a short distance away.

'I didn't think statues could eat,' murmured Ed.

'They can't. But those servant types just cannot help themselves. They're usually clustered around the base of Albert's plinth, gazing lovingly up at him, and naturally they follow him wherever he goes. They're simply trying to give the impression that there's a big feast going on.'

Ed quickly saw that this was correct. The waiters kept rearranging the items, carrying them to and fro, between the two tables. The two larger statues were taking absolutely no notice of their antics.

'Who's the bloke sitting beside Victoria?' asked Ed. 'Is it her dad?'

'No, that's her husband, Prince Albert. They were actually the same age but of course, *his* statue depicts him much later in life. It can be a little confusing.' Sherlock pointed to the tethered horse. 'He's ridden over from Charlotte Square. It's always the first thing he does when the clock strikes twelve. The Calling is a very special event for both of them. Albert died in 1861, you see, and Victoria lived until 1901. She mourned him all the rest of her life. This is the one time in the entire year when they can actually be together again.'

'I see. Why's he all *green*?'

'Oh, that's just verdigris.'

'It's what?'

'It's caused by oxidisation… exposure to the elements.'

'I don't really understand.'

'Well, it's like rust. It's simply the way bronze rusts.'

'But… you're made of bronze, aren't you? And you're not that colour.'

'Well, I haven't been around as long as he has.'

'The Colonel's bronze and he…'

'Some statues are regularly treated with a clear varnish to prevent the oxidisation from happening.'

'So why doesn't somebody…?'

'Has anybody ever told you you ask an awful lot of questions?' snapped Sherlock irritably. 'Now hush for a moment.'

The Gormley was leaning politely forward to speak to the Queen. She lifted her head and looked in Sherlock's direction. At first she smiled, but when she spotted Ed, the smile quickly faded. However, she nodded and the Gormley turned back and gestured for Sherlock and Ed to approach, before stepping politely aside.

'My dear Mr Holmes,' said Victoria, as they reached the table. 'How lovely to see you again. To what do I owe this rare pleasure?'

Sherlock bowed politely. 'Your Majesty, please

forgive the interruption.' He turned slightly and bowed to Prince Albert. 'I know how precious your time together is. But as you can see…' He waved a hand at Ed. '… I have a bit of a problem on my hands.'

'A sovv-dy,' said Prince Albert, in a strange Germanic accent. 'A leedle human poy. And nod azleep. How very peculiar!'

'Indeed,' agreed Sherlock. 'I shan't bore you with the details of how he came to be here. I will only mention that he is suffering from amnesia and knows very little about who he is or where he's from. I have been charged with the task of finding out all about him and returning him to his home.'

'Charged by whom?' asked Victoria, disdainfully. 'No, no, let me guess. By Charles, of course, who else?'

'Umm… yes, I'm afraid so.' Sherlock looked apologetic. 'I can assure you, Your Majesty, in my opinion there's only one person who has the right to govern us statues, and that is you, but I fear the majority has chosen him. He gave me the order and I had little option but to obey him.'

'Zat man,' growled Albert. 'How I vud like to punch him! Ride on de noze!'

'No Bertie, that would be most uncivilized,' said Victoria primly. 'We shan't descend to that level. As long as he stays away from Leith Walk, he's welcome to call himself whatever he wishes. King of Edinburgh… Emperor of Siam, it's of no consequence to me.' She focused her attention on Ed. 'So, boy, you have certainly stumbled onto something unusual, haven't you? How does it feel to be the first softie ever to witness this incredible event?'

Ed tried to smile. 'It… feels really weird,' he said. 'Er… Your Majesty. I'm… still like… y'know, trying to get my head round it.'

Victoria seemed puzzled by the answer. She looked at Sherlock as though seeking a translation.

'He says, Your Majesty, that he's somewhat discombobulated by the situation and is struggling to come to terms with it,' added Sherlock.

'Ah. I understand.' Victoria smiled sympathetically at Ed, as though she really did know exactly how he felt. She returned her gaze to Sherlock. 'And how may I assist you with this matter, Mr Holmes?'

'Well, Your Majesty, this is an unusual situation, which I feel requires unusual measures in order to resolve it. I would therefore respectfully request your permission to undertake a secret mission. I wish to leave Edinburgh for a while, in order to solve the case.'

Victoria and Albert exchanged puzzled looks.

'Such a sing is possible?' gasped Albert. 'Surely not?'

'I believe it is, sir. It's never been attempted, of course, indeed it's strictly forbidden, but over the past couple of years, I have been working with Dr Clerk Maxwell on an apparatus that should allow me to do exactly that.'

Albert looked puzzled. 'Clerk Maxvell?' he muttered.

'Yes, you know, dear, the scientist chappie,' explained Victoria. 'The one who was supposed to have inspired Einstein?'

Albert grunted. 'Science!' he muttered. 'Who can get inderested in zat?'

'He also invented colour photography,' added Victoria. 'I seem to remember reading the article to you when you were on your sickbed. You… you were very interested, at the time. Terribly ill, of course, but still interested…'

She looked suddenly very sad and so did Albert.

'My poor dollink,' he murmured.

'Oh, Bertie…' The two of them sat staring into each other's eyes and Ed felt suddenly as though he ought to be somewhere else. Sherlock gave a polite cough and Victoria managed to drag her gaze away from that of her husband. 'This… apparatus of yours, Mr Holmes?' she asked. 'It has been tested?'

'No, not yet, Your Majesty. But at last year's Calling, Dr Clerk Maxwell and I discussed the possibility of actually trying it out. This would seem to be an ideal opportunity.' Sherlock frowned. 'Of course, such a thing would be considered highly improper by King Charles. He's very… old fashioned in his views. He'd doubtless consider our method a form of witchcraft. Hopefully, if the technique works, I'll be there and back within a few hours and nobody will be any the wiser… but… if for any reason my plan should be discovered…'

'Yes?'

'It would be very helpful if I could claim that the mission was sanctioned by Queen Victoria herself.'

'I see.'

'The king wouldn't dare go against you, Your Majesty. He knows only too well that there's already a strong faction of statues who would prefer to see you as our rightful monarch.'

Victoria frowned. She looked at her husband. 'What do you think, Bertie?'

'I sink anysing zat puts that bully's nose out of joint is fine vis me,' said Albert. 'I zay go for it!'

'Very well, my dear. I shall, of course, follow your excellent advice.' Victoria gestured to the Gormley. 'You, there! Fetch me a pen and paper. I shall put it in writing.'

The Gormley stood for a moment, looking vaguely confused. Then he stumbled off towards the shopping mall, pulling a bunch of keys from the pocket of his hoodie as he did so. Victoria rolled her eyes. 'One simply cannot get the staff these days,' she observed. She returned her attention to Sherlock. 'So, Mr Holmes, when will you attempt this ground-breaking plan?'

'Just as soon as it can be organised, your Majesty. We have, after all, a window of less than twenty-four hours.'

'Well, I'm sure you're no stranger to action and adventure,' said Victoria. 'I was such a fan of your short stories. I used to read them in the *Strand Magazine*. After

Bertie left me, they were one of my few consolations. They helped me pass the lonely and fretful hours.' She and Albert looked at each other once again.

'My dollink!' he said.

'Oh, Bertie!' she replied.

Once again, Ed felt vaguely embarrassed by their evident affection for each other. He decided to try and make some conversation, if only to break the awful silence.

'Er… excuse me your… Your Majesty.'

Victoria turned to look at him, a disapproving expression on her face. 'Yes, boy?' she said.

'I… I was just wondering… I've seen so many statues since I got here. There must have been like hundreds of them in Parliament Square. But… well, you're the only woman I've seen. Why's that?'

Victoria looked decidedly irked by this comment. 'Because history has always been in the grip of the men of the world,' she said grumpily. 'No matter that there have been hundreds of prominent females deserving of commemoration, they have been repeatedly overlooked. Where, pray, is the statue of Flora McDonald? Hmm? Or Mary Queen of Scots? Or Catriona McCallum?'

Ed could only shrug. He'd never heard of any of them, but he supposed they must be famous for something. 'I… I really don't know,' he said.

'Well, they're certainly not to be found in Edinburgh! And why, please tell me, does Charles have pride of place in Parliament Square, while I, a Queen for more than fifty years, have to be content with this wretched spot in front of a… a shopping arcade? Does that strike you as fair?'

'I… I suppose not,' muttered Ed. 'So… you really *are* the only one?'

'Well, there's me, and there's some poor unnamed South African woman with a weeping child up on Fountainbridge. That's the kind of esteem in which womankind is held in this city, young man. But what can you expect when all the sculptors are male? When the businessmen who paid for the monuments are male? When the people who write the history books are male?'

'Well, I…'

'Mind you, I sometimes wonder if it's a conspiracy against me. Why is it, I ask myself, that Charles stands there in Parliament Square, the same colour as the day when he was first placed upon that podium?'

'Oh, I think it's because he's made of…'

'And yet, my dear beloved husband… my Bertie… well, look at him! He's the colour of a ripe cucumber!'

'Now, now, dollink,' said Albert, sympathetically. 'Don't go getting yourself all virked up!'

'I can't help it, Bertie. It's really not fair. It's not good for you. Your poor joints, you can hardly move these days. You said yourself, every step is agony. How long before you seize up altogether? How long before…?'

Her tirade was interrupted by the return of the Gormley, carrying a notepad and biro. Ed couldn't help noticing that the pink notepad had the words 'Hello Kitty' printed on the cover beside the image of a cartoon cat. Victoria regarded it sullenly.

'Is this *really* the best you could find?' she snapped.

The Gormley bowed his head. 'I'm sorry, yer Madge. S'all I could get at short notice.'

'Oh, very well. I suppose it will have to suffice.' Victoria cleared a space on the table, opened the notebook and began to write laboriously on the lined paper. At one point she paused and looked up at her husband. 'Bertie, how do you spell "solemnly"?' And he patiently spelt it out for her while she followed his instructions. When she had finally finished, she signed her name with a flourish, tore off the sheet of paper and handed it to Sherlock. 'Will that do for your purposes?' she asked.

Sherlock scanned the note for a moment and then smiled. 'That is perfect,' he said. 'My eternal gratitude, Your Majesty.' He bowed his head, then folded the paper in half and slipped it inside his coat. 'May I enquire what your plans are for this evening? Will you be visiting the Agon?'

'We will not,' said Victoria primly. 'All those pompous males braying about their so-called accomplishments! The last time we attended, Robbie Burns read out what was supposed to be a comic poem. It was unspeakably vulgar! We were not amused. No, Bertie and I shall make the most of our time together. We shall stroll out across the Meadows and observe the sun setting behind Arthur's Seat. It was always one of our favourite views.'

'Ve had many heppy times looking at zat view,' murmured Albert. 'Chust me and Vigtoria.'

Victoria turned back to her husband and took his hands in hers.

'Oh Bertie,' she murmured.

'My dollink,' he said.

Once again, they were gazing rapturously into each other's eyes, so Sherlock took the opportunity to grab Ed's arm and lead him away across the road to the far pavement, where Bobby was still waiting for them, his tail wagging insistently

'Are they always that soppy?' whispered Ed.

'I'm afraid so,' said Sherlock. 'I suppose that's true love for you.'

'And... is it right, what you just said? That you can leave Edinburgh?'

'I believe so. But first, we need to set things up.' Sherlock glanced quickly up and down the street then reached inside his coat and pulled out a mobile phone. It was one of the latest mini tablet-sized models but it still looked tiny in his huge metal hands. He keyed in some numbers, waited a moment and then spoke. 'James? Where are you? Good. Look, it's on for tonight. All systems are go. Yes, that's what I said. All systems are go! I'll explain everything when I see you. Where are you now? I see. Well, make your excuses and get over to the lab with all speed. Can you meet me there at… say around six? Yes, I do mean six AM! There will be two of us, by the way. No, no, not another statue. No, I haven't told anyone else about the Anomaly. As I said, I'll explain when I see you. Bye!'

He signed off and slipped the phone back into his pocket.

'I didn't know you were allowed phones,' said Ed.

'We're not,' hissed Sherlock. 'So forget you ever saw that. But James and I needed a way to get in touch easily. When you only have one day a year every moment is precious. There wouldn't be time to send him a written invitation, would there?' He started walking back the way they had come and Ed followed him. Bobby trotted happily along in their wake.

'So you've got permission to leave Edinburgh,' murmured Ed. 'Where exactly are you going?'

'I'm not going anywhere,' Sherlock corrected him. '*We're* going. As in, you're coming with me.'

'Oh, I see. But where?'

'To Manchester, of course. The fact that you're a native of the city is about the only thing we're reasonably sure of. We'll find out what happened to you to make you lose your memory, I'll get you back where you belong and I'll return here in time for the changeover.'

'I see…' Ed felt vaguely disappointed. 'Couldn't I… couldn't I come back with you?' he asked. 'Once I know who I am. Just until the Calling is over?'

Sherlock glared at him. 'Why on earth would you want to do that?'

'Well, I was kind of beginning to enjoy being here… learning about all this crazy stuff. I mean, maybe once we know who I am, we could come back for the rest of the Calling. I could go to the Agon and everything and then tomorrow, after it's all over and you're back on your plinth, I'd just leave for Manchester on the next train or something.'

'I wouldn't be in such a big hurry to come back here if I was you,' said Sherlock, mysteriously.

'Why not?'

'Because of Charlie.'

Now Ed was completely baffled. 'What about him?' he said.

'My boy, I know him better than you do. I know how his mind works. You see, he won't like the fact that you know all about the Calling. He'll be thinking to himself, "What if that boy were to tell others about it?" As in, other humans.'

'I've already promised him I won't do that,' Ed assured him. 'And besides, who would believe me? They'd think I'd gone barmy.'

'Perhaps. But that won't mean anything to him,' murmured Sherlock. 'He's a paranoid. He'd go to any lengths to keep the Calling a secret. And what did the Colonel say when he brought you to me? That Charlie had been talking about chopping somebody's head off? That wouldn't have been *your* head, by any chance?'

'Umm… well yes, it was, actually.'

'That's what I deduced. You may think that you got

away with that, but once Charlie gets an idea into his mind, he never gives up on it.'

Ed stopped in his tracks for a moment, a hand at his own throat. Then he hurried after the detective.

'You're not saying that he'd…?'

'I'm not saying anything. I just think it would be a lot better for you if I return to Edinburgh empty-handed and tell Charlie that I… lost you.'

'Couldn't you tell him the truth? That you took me there in your special machine?'

Now Sherlock was shaking his head. 'Oh no,' he said. 'Absolutely not. I don't ever want Charlie to find out about the Anomaly… that's what we call it, by the way, our apparatus. The Anomaly. No, if Charlie found out about that, there's no telling what he might do. Like I said before, to him it would be pure witchcraft. He'd certainly have it destroyed. Or worse still, he'd use it himself for some wicked purpose. No, trust me on this, it's best if we stick to my story.'

'But… if you say you lost me… won't that make you look a bit… useless?'

Sherlock laughed dismissively. 'I'm not worried about that! Charlie already thinks that about me anyway. Trust me, I know the man. This will just ensure that you're safe. And that of course, is my primary objective. So I'm taking you to Manchester, just as soon as I can organise it. And for you, it's best if it's a one way ticket.'

'OK, I suppose you know what you're doing. One thing though…'

'Yes?'

'What will it look like?'

Sherlock scowled down at him. 'Whatever do you mean?'

'What are people in Manchester going to think when they see a kid walking along the street with a nine foot tall statue?'

Sherlock frowned. 'That's actually a very good point,' he said. 'I hadn't considered that.' He thought for a moment and then smiled. 'Luckily, you've overlooked one of my most celebrated skills.'

'Oh yeah. What's that?'

Sherlock smiled. 'As well as being a brilliant detective, I'm also a master of disguise,' he said.

THIRTEEN

Incognito

S herlock stepped out from the changing cubicle and stood in front of Ed, a questioning look on his oddly transformed face. 'Well?' he said. 'How do I look?'

Ed didn't really know how to answer that question. He considered saying what he actually *thought*, that the great detective looked 'really weird,' but decided that wouldn't be helpful. So instead he just nodded thoughtfully and said, 'Hmm. Yeah…' Bobby wagged his tail, but even he seemed puzzled.

'Hmm, yeah? Is that all you've got to say?'

They were in a huge department store called Jenners (just one more place that Sherlock happened to have a key for.) They were in the menswear department and Sherlock was demonstrating his 'disguise' – or at least, his attempt to pass for a human being. For a start, he'd managed to find what must have been the biggest grey raincoat ever made, which he was wearing on top of his bronze clothing – and he'd also found a wide-brimmed black hat, which fitted neatly over the top of his deerstalker. His huge hands were enclosed in leather gloves, though to actually get them on, he'd had to take a pair of scissors and cut them open from the wrists to the middle of his palms. Of course, the colour of his bronze 'skin' had proved to be a real problem, so he'd picked up some cosmetics on the way up here, a large tube of foundation makeup and some rouge, both of which he'd plastered onto his face in an attempt to make him look more 'human,' though the corpse-like pallor he'd achieved just looked really strange. The outfit was completed by a pair of aviator-style sunglasses, because there was no way in the world he was ever going to be able to make his metal eyes look real.

'You look... different,' said Ed.

Sherlock scowled. 'That isn't a proper answer. The question is, can I pass for a human, looking like this?'

'I... I suppose so,' muttered Ed. 'A really... odd-looking human. It's just that you're so... *big*.'

'I can't do anything about my height,' reasoned Sherlock. 'But there must surely be *some* tall people around Manchester?'

'Maybe... basketball players?' offered Ed.

'Well, it'll have to do. We don't have an awful lot of time at our disposal.' Sherlock reached under the real coat and pulled out his pocket watch. 'We need to be going,' he said. 'We've already wasted enough time on this.' He slipped the makeup into the pockets of his raincoat and led the way back through the departments and down the stairs to the entrance. He let Ed and Bobby out onto the street and they watched as he locked up and reset the burglar alarm.

'How does it work with the keys?' asked Ed. 'I mean, you surely can't have one for every building in Edinburgh.'

'No, but between us, we have keys for all of the useful places,' said Sherlock. 'Sometimes, if we need one for a particular place, we can simply borrow it from somebody else. And on certain occasions, we have even been known to make duplicates.'

They soon found themselves walking alongside Princes Street Gardens again and heading across Waverley Bridge. They passed a couple of white stone statues walking the other way, two elderly men in wigs and frock coats who had been deep in conversation as they approached, but who stared in open amazement as Sherlock and Ed went by.

'Morning,' muttered Ed self-consciously but Sherlock just ignored them. He appeared to be deep in thought. Once again, Ed wondered what people in the real world were going to make of the enormous shambling figure beside him.

'So tell me more about this machine you've built,' he suggested.

'Hmm?' Sherlock looked down at him as though

annoyed at the interruption. 'I can assure you, I have had nothing to do with its creation. It's James' invention. I merely inspired him.'

'James?'

'James Clerk Maxwell. He's Edinburgh's most famous…'

'Physicist. Yes, David Livingstone mentioned him to me. So, how did you inspire him exactly?'

'Well, I happened to mention an idea to him at one of the Callings and by the following year, he'd pretty much worked out how to make it a reality.'

Ed nodded. 'What was the idea?'

'Well, if you really want to know, I merely said how dreary travel must be for humans and wouldn't it be wonderful if you could just step through a door in Edinburgh and arrive instantly, anywhere else in the world.'

'Wow! And that's what this machine can do?'

'Hopefully.' Ed couldn't help noticing that Sherlock kept his gaze fixed on the way ahead. 'That's… pretty much the gist of it…'

Ed sensed that he was being vague. 'Hang on a minute. Didn't you tell Queen Victoria that it hadn't been tested yet?'

'Erm… well, actually, I wasn't completely honest with her. We did er… have a bit of a test, only two years ago.'

Ed felt suddenly rather suspicious. 'What do you mean? A bit of a test?'

'Well, we erm… we sent a statue through the door. Just a little statue of a… a cherub. Silly little creature, really, of no great importance. He happened to mention that he wasn't enjoying his life in Edinburgh any more and he fancied a change of climate, so we er… offered to give him one. Of course, it isn't an actual door, you understand, it's more of a portal. An opening into another dimension.'

'Right… and where did you send this… this cherub?'

'Well, we sent him to India, actually. He said he'd always wanted to see the place, so we thought "Why not?"' That's as good a test destination as any.'

Ed was beginning to get a bad feeling about this.

'And… did he get there?'

'Oh yes, we're fairly sure he did. Of course, we did warn him before he left to make sure he was back by midnight… it's a bit like Cinderella when you think about it. You know, the glass slipper and all that? Only… well… it could be that he got confused by the time difference, and…'

'And what?' Ed prompted him.

'Well, he… he's not actually back yet.'

'Yet? But that was two years ago!'

'Umm… true. We're not sure what happened. It could be that he just preferred it there, or… maybe he didn't get back to the portal in time and sort of… froze. But James has made quite a few adjustments since then, so…'

'Wait!' Ed stopped in his tracks. 'I'm not sure about this,' he said. 'It sounds dangerous.'

'Not at all!' Sherlock paused and turned back to look at him. 'Do you really think I'd be offering to go with you if I thought it was dangerous?'

'You might. You're supposed to be quite brave aren't you?'

'Well, yes, but I'm not foolhardy. Besides, I have complete trust in James. His is one of the greatest minds of the nineteenth century. Oh, if they'd had your kind of technology back when he was alive, who knows what he might have accomplished? Every year the Calling comes around and he's there with another amazing idea, all ready to go.'

Ed got the impression that Sherlock was deliberately trying to change the subject, so he didn't pursue the point but he couldn't help feeling worried. He wondered what had happened to the cherub. Was there now an unexplained little statue in the middle of a high street in Mumbai? And was he still able to come alive for just one day of the year?

He and Sherlock had stepped off the main street now and were wandering along a wide, straight avenue with a row of trees on either side of them. The way ahead was divided by a white line along its centre, half for pedestrians, half for bicycles. Ed was astonished to see that a human on a bicycle was slumped asleep in his saddle, right in the middle of the track, his front light still flashing rhythmically, even though it was now broad daylight. More weirdly, his bike had somehow remained upright, supported by nothing more than fresh air. Ed stared in disbelief. 'How is that even possible?' he asked. 'Why doesn't he lose his balance?'

'Just another of the wonders of the Calling,' said Sherlock. 'You see, from midnight, human time simply freezes. That chap was probably on his way home from a party. At midnight tonight he'll just carry on pedalling to his destination.'

'It's incredible,' observed Ed.

'It is, but we statues take it for granted now. The real mystery to me is that you are able to move and talk and breathe at all. It's against all the laws of reason. If we had more time it's something I'd like to investigate in more detail. What is it about you that makes you different to every other human in Edinburgh?'

Ed shrugged. 'I don't know,' he admitted. 'The Colonel reckons it's something to do with me losing my memory.'

'He could be right, I suppose. I expect James will have a theory about it. He's good at that kind of logical thinking.'

'Better than you?' asked Ed, surprised.

'Oh no, not better than me. Nobody's better than me.'

Ed laughed at that and Sherlock allowed himself a smile. 'I know it can come across as arrogance, but I feel I'm merely stating facts.'

'So how do you stand it?' Ed asked him.

'How do I stand what?'

'Being stuck on that plinth, all year round, not able to move. Just waiting for the one day when you can *do* some stuff. I... I can't imagine what that must feel like. Doesn't it make you want to... scream and shout? What if...?' He thought for a moment. 'What if you get a really bad itch and you need to scratch it? That must be awful.'

Sherlock shrugged. 'It is simply the statue's lot in life,' he said. 'We all have the same limitations. Think what it must be like for the other statues around the world! They *never* get to move. As far as I am aware, they don't even have thoughts and feelings, like we do. And at least we have the whole year to anticipate the Calling. You know, I suppose it's a little bit like being a butterfly. All that time they spend getting ready for their big day. They are eggs, they are grubs, they are locked in a cocoon... until finally, finally the time comes and they have just that one summer's day to spread their wings and fly. And then, almost as soon as it's begun, it's all over for them. At least we get to spread our wings again and again.'

'But if you had the chance... I mean, if somebody could make it happen... wouldn't you prefer to be human?'

Sherlock opened his mouth to reply, but broke off as an abrupt hissing sound rent the air. He reacted instinctively, grabbing Ed, twisting around and pulling him close in behind him. An instant later something hit Sherlock full in the stomach before shattering noisily into fragments and flying off in all directions. Ed looked down in astonishment to see scraps of splintered wood falling to the ground and then he saw a sharp metal object clatter onto the tarmac and he realised what it was. An arrowhead! It dawned on him that somebody had just tried to kill him and that if Sherlock hadn't intercepted the shot, that arrow would now be sticking out from Ed's chest. He was aware of Bobby crouching by his feet, his little teeth bared, his ears flat against his head, an angry snarl coming out of him.

'Stay behind me,' snapped Sherlock, looking frantically this way and that. Ed peered fearfully out from under the detective's arm and caught a glimpse of something moving in the trees, a metal figure standing half-concealed by foliage, some twenty feet away.

'There!' yelled Ed, pointing, and now he could see the figure in more detail: a naked bronze statue who, even as Ed stared in horror, was pulling back the string of a wooden bow for another shot.

'I see you, you coward!' roared Sherlock and an instant later a second arrow careened off his shoulder and went spinning end over end, behind him.

Sherlock started towards the Gormley, but then wheeled around with a curse as a clatter broke the silence from somewhere behind them. Now Ed glimpsed a second Gormley, armed, like his companion, with a bow. He had just popped up from behind the cover of a metal litterbin and his elbow had accidentally made contact with the lid. He had the bowstring pulled back as far as it would go. There was another hiss and Ed was horribly aware of a blur of colour right in front of his face – but then Sherlock's gloved hand actually snatched the arrow out of thin air and dashed it to the ground, seconds before it could hit its intended target. Ed's heart seemed to stop momentarily in his chest and his skin crawled with terror.

The full reality of the situation finally dawned on him. The Gormleys were trying to kill him! But why? What had he done to deserve it? There was a moment of deep silence as he and Sherlock stood there debating what to do, unsure now which way to face; then Sherlock pushed Ed towards a narrow alleyway, leading off the main thoroughfare to their left, and he shouted, 'Run, boy! I'll be right behind you.'

Ed needed no second bidding. He took off along the alley with all the speed he could muster and Sherlock followed right on his heels, keeping as close as he could to provide some cover. Bobby scampered after them, barking excitedly. A third arrow hit Sherlock square in the back and this time it actually managed to pierce his bronze skin, but he and Ed kept on running for all they were worth and when they finally dared to glance back, the already distant mouth of the alley was empty and nobody appeared to be following them.

'All right,' said Sherlock. 'I don't think they're

following us.' They slowed to a walk. Ed was already out of breath, but Sherlock showed no sign of that and it occurred to Ed that if a statue didn't need to breathe, running wasn't going to be a problem for him. Bobby, too, seemed unaffected by the race. He trotted along behind his companions, his tail wagging.

'What... what was that all about?' gasped Ed. 'They... they were trying to kill me.'

'It's exactly as I feared,' murmured Sherlock. He reached around behind himself, grabbed the end of the arrow and pulled it free with a grunt. He looked at it for a moment and then dashed it to the ground with a curse. 'Those two Gormleys work for Charlie. He must have sent them after you.'

'But... he... he *pardoned* me!'

Sherlock looked unconvinced. 'Then he's clearly changed his mind. Was it *his* idea in the first place? To pardon you?'

'Well, no... not really. David kind of tricked him into it, so...'

'David?'

'David Livingstone. Charlie wanted to... well, he wanted to have my head chopped off but... David made the others vote on it and...'

'Well, there you are then.' Sherlock brushed scraps of splintered wood from his coat with a huge gloved hand. 'Charlie's not a man to take being bested lightly. He wants you silenced. He'll have instructed those two minions of his to come after you.' He studied the top of the alley in silence for a moment, his expression grim. 'All the more reason to get you away from here before those two have a chance to regroup.'

'I don't understand,' said Ed. 'I promised him I wouldn't tell anyone about all this.'

Sherlock reached down to place a huge hand on Ed's shoulder. 'It doesn't matter what you promised,' he murmured. 'Charlie dances to a different drum.' He glanced quickly around. 'We're not far from the lab now. But, we're going to have to take a roundabout route. The last thing we need is for those Gormleys to work out where we're headed. I shudder to think what might happen if they ever reported back to Charlie about the Anomaly.' He had another look around and seemed satisfied. 'Come on,' he said and started walking. 'Keep your eyes peeled for those two villains. If you see anything, just shout.'

They hurried along the alleyway and Sherlock started to make a bewildering series of changes to the route, cutting left and right, doubling back on himself, unlocking doors to pass though entire buildings, then locking another door behind them, occasionally stopping to look and listen for any signs that they might be followed. Finally, when they had been doing this for more than half an hour, he produced a key to an innocuous-looking little doorway and opened it up. He led Ed and Bobby inside, pausing to lock the door behind him and keeping watch for a moment through a small glass panel before he was entirely satisfied.

'All right,' he said, at last. 'I think we've lost them. This way.' He led Ed up a long flight of stairs to the first floor, then along a corridor where they passed a whole series of glass-fronted rooms, each of which appeared to be fitted with lab equipment of all shapes and sizes – test tubes, Bunsen burners, microscopes and computers. After they had gone some distance, Sherlock paused outside a frosted glass doorway and rapped upon it with his knuckles, in a curiously complicated pattern. They waited in silence for a few moments and finally there was the sound of several bolts being drawn and the door creaked slowly open. A tall bronze statue stood in the opening, gazing out at them, a look of mild irritation on his heavily bearded face. He was slightly silhouetted against a pulsing red glow coming from behind him. He registered the detective's odd appearance and stared at him in bewilderment.

'Sherlock, what in the name of mercy have you done to yourself?' he cried in a Scottish accent. 'You look ridiculous.'

'It's a disguise,' Sherlock assured him. 'So I can pass for a human.'

'Really? Let's hope the humans have a sense of humour,' muttered James Clerk Maxwell. He took a pocket watch from his waistcoat and held it out so that Sherlock could see the time displayed on it.

'You're late,' he said. 'You know I can't abide tardiness of any kind.'

Sherlock smiled. 'Sorry, but I do have a good excuse.' He stepped aside, revealing Ed, who had been standing behind him.

'Galloping gravy!' said James. 'Is that what I think it is?'

'I'm afraid so,' said Sherlock.

'Well, don't just stand there! The two of you had better come inside.'

FOURTEEN

The Anomaly

Ed gazed apprehensively around the small, cramped room. A complicated arrangement of electronic equipment had been set up on a workbench along the back wall. There were digital displays, several computers, dials, switches and various other bits and pieces, none of which meant anything to him. At the centre of the display was a large circular glass dish, which was emitting a pulsing red light and a constant low humming sound.

On entering the room, Bobby had been delighted to discover that James had a dog with him too, a ragged little bronze terrier who James had introduced as Toby and the two dogs were happily rubbing noses and sniffing at each other in the time-honoured fashion of such creatures all over the world. Ed had been left to his own devices for the moment, while Sherlock and

James had an intense conversation at the back of the room, keeping their voices hushed so Ed wouldn't overhear them. James appeared to be intrigued by his human visitor. He couldn't stop staring at Ed and kept asking Sherlock questions, listening to the replies and then nodding, as though evaluating them. Eventually, he seemed satisfied and he approached Ed, smiling, his hands in his metal pockets.

'A belated welcome to you,' he said, in a refined Edinburgh accent. 'Mr Holmes has fully appraised me of your unfortunate situation. I have to say I am fascinated. I've never had the opportunity to talk to a human before. Indeed, if there was only more time, I would love to study you.'

'Erm…' Ed felt slightly uncomfortable at this. 'Study me, how?'

'Well, there are a lot of questions that are just crying out to be answered,' said James. 'Why should you be the first softie in history to resist sleeping through the Calling? Why, after all these years, does the honour fall to you? What is so very *different* about you?'

'Search me,' muttered Ed.

For a moment James looked as though he might actually be thinking of doing exactly that. But he seemed to dismiss the idea. 'If Sherlock was planning on bringing you back with him, I'd definitely have a whole list of questions for you. But he assures me that, for you at least, this is to be a one-way trip. Such a pity. What a missed opportunity to further our knowledge of humankind.' He sighed then gestured to the banks of electronic equipment. 'So, what do you think of our little brainchild?' he asked.

'It's er… very… red,' murmured Ed and James chuckled delightedly.

'It is indeed,' he said. 'Red! I'd never thought of it like that.' He turned to look at Sherlock. 'So, where exactly is it you need to go?'

'It's in Manchester,' said Sherlock. 'You have your mobile?'

'Of course.' James reached into his pocket and brought out an identical phone to the one Sherlock used. 'Never without it.'

'Bring up Google maps while I look for the postcode,' suggested Sherlock. He took out his pipe and tapped it. The curved Perspex screen slid down from the peak of his cap. He peered intently at nothing for a moment and then read the postcode aloud to James, who dutifully tapped it into his own phone. Then James walked over to the bench, picked up a lead that was plugged into one of the computers and connected the other end to his mobile. Almost instantly, a blurred map appeared on the screen. It focused itself and there was the familiar red marker indicating their destination.

'*The Peveril of the Peak*,' read Sherlock, looking over James' shoulder. '*Fine ales. Table football.* It's not a lot to go on but it's the best clue we have.'

Ed chuckled. 'Google maps are great, aren't they?' he said.

'Yes, and perfectly suited to our needs,' chuckled James, with evident pride. He studied the screen for a few moments. 'Of course, for the moment we're only using existing technology. Wait till you see what happens when we patch it in to the Anomaly.' He waved a hand at the equipment, then studied the screen again. 'The main road is a bit too public for my liking,' he observed. 'We need somewhere where your arrival is less likely to be observed by passers-by.'

Sherlock nodded. 'Switch to street view,' he suggested, 'and we'll look for the best place.'

As Ed watched in amazement, the pub itself appeared on the screen and it was just as he'd seen it in his vision, a small two-storey affair, completely clad in green tiles, pea green on the ground floor and a paler shade above. The name of the pub was spelled out in tiles on a brown band that ran right around the building between the two floors and it was also on a large painted sign above the main door. James used the mouse to track effortlessly around the side of the building to the back of it. 'Ah look,' he said, 'there's a little walled yard at the back with a gate set into it. That should be the ideal spot.'

'Perfect,' said Sherlock. 'Lock onto those co-ordinates.'

James tapped some keys and the computer made a brief beeping sound, as though announcing it understood.

'Locked on,' said James. 'Well, getting you there should be no problem at all. But what do you want me to do about bringing you back?' He frowned. 'I take it you *are* coming back?'

'Of course I am.' Sherlock touched his pipe and the screen slid silently back out of sight into the peak of his hat. 'At least, I hope to be. Once I know what's happening, I'll text you a postcode and a time,' he said, slipping the pipe and the phone back into his pockets. 'Obviously, you'll have to keep an eye on things here. I'm afraid it means that you're going to miss the Agon.'

'That's no great loss,' said James. 'I swore the last time I went I would never do it again, not after hearing Sir Walter droning through one of his interminable ballads. Besides…' He gestured to a pile of notes littering the workbench. 'I've got plenty of reading to keep me occupied.' He leaned closer as if to reveal a secret. 'I'm working on another little modification for the Anomaly,' he said. 'If I stick at it till late tonight, I reckon I could have it all ready to go for next year's Calling.' He grinned mischievously. 'It's a voice activation module. Once it's installed, it means you'll be able to simply tell the machine exactly where you want to go… and it will take you there in the blink of an eye.'

'Sounds good,' agreed Sherlock. 'But look, we mustn't leave things too late. There has to be enough time for us to get back to our respective plinths. You don't want to get frozen in here, do you?'

'Good point. Same goes for you, of course. If *I* froze at least I'd be in the right city. How would they ever explain you being in an entirely different location altogether?'

'They'd probably blame it on drunken students,' said Sherlock. 'That's what they generally do with these things.'

'Er... about the... Anomaly,' interrupted Ed.

The two statues turned to look at him. 'Yes?' asked James.

'It is ... well, it is safe and everything? Isn't it? Only, Sherlock told me about the cherub. You know, the little statue you sent to India...?'

James threw an accusing look at Sherlock. 'Oh you did, did you?' he growled. 'That was useful.'

'I merely mentioned it in passing,' said Sherlock.

'Hmm.' For a moment James looked rather annoyed, but then he forced a smile and turned back to face Ed. 'Well, yes, that *was* rather unfortunate,' he admitted. 'Something happened with that experiment that we hadn't fully accounted for... but, we've had another two Callings since then so that little hiccup has been well and truly taken care of.'

'A little hiccup?' asked Ed. 'Is that what you call it?'

'Yes... just a wee... complication. But it's all fine and dandy now. Seriously, you'd be in more danger crossing the road! The Anomaly is... well, it's the future of travel. Just think of the tedium everyone endures when they're going from A to B, even in this day and age! I mean, how long did it take you to get from Manchester to Edinburgh?'

Ed shrugged. 'I was asleep the whole way,' he said.

'Well, fair enough, but some people can't sleep on trains, can they? With our invention you simply step through a door and you've arrived at your destination. Instantly! Forgotten something? No problem, you can just nip back and pick it up, no matter what the distance. Of course, the only fly in the ointment is, how do we tell the world about it?'

Sherlock frowned. 'I'd personally prefer to keep the invention for the sole use of us statues. I really don't think humankind can be trusted to use it responsibly. They'd probably employ it as some kind of weapon.'

'There's something I don't quite understand,' said Ed.

The two statues looked at him. 'What's the problem?' asked James.

'Well, I'm trying to understand. Time has kind of stopped here in Edinburgh, right?'

James frowned. 'Not stopped exactly. But it's running in a different dimension.'

'Yes, but it must still be moving forward normally in Manchester, so if we go there now… will it still be today… or will it be tomorrow?'

James looked thoughtful at this. 'Well, now there's a question. Of course, you must remember, that time is simply a concept created by man. And The Anomaly, of course, calibrates itself to the two different time spheres. So people in Manchester will still be interacting with you in real time. And it won't be today *or* tomorrow, but… something in between.' He noticed Ed's bemused expression. 'Well, put it this way. I'm sure you've read Stephen Hawking's *A Brief History of Time*?'

'No,' said Ed. 'Sorry.' He thought for a moment. 'But I've read *The Time Machine*,' he offered.

'Yes, but that's not quite the same thing,' said James. 'That's science fiction. This is science *fact*. If I had a couple of hours to spare, I'm sure I could explain it to you in a way you'd understand, but…'

'We don't *have* the luxury of time,' interrupted Sherlock. 'We need to go.'

'Yes, of course.' James smiled at Ed. 'You'll just have to trust me,' he concluded and clapped his hands together as if to end the conversation. 'Well, we're all ready to proceed. If you would like to take up your positions?'

'Certainly.' Sherlock put a huge metal hand on Ed's shoulder and guided him to the centre of the room, where a crude X had been made on the tiled floor with two lengths of gaffer tape. Bobby attempted to go with them but James raised a hand. 'No, Bobby, you stay here with Toby,' he said in a firm tone. 'This is no job for a wee doggie.'

Bobby stood there, looking up at Ed and Sherlock, a pleading expression on his face.

'Can't he come with us?' asked Ed.

'How would we ever explain him?' asked Sherlock. 'It'll be tough enough explaining *me*.' He shook his head. 'Sorry, Bobby, you wait here, there's a good lad. We'll be back before you know it.'

Bobby looked disappointed but went obediently back to stand with his canine companion. Sherlock moved Ed slightly to the left, so his feet were centred on the strips of tape. 'Now, I want you to keep absolutely still until I tell you it's safe to move,' he said.

'Er… OK,' said Ed, warily. 'It won't… hurt, will it?'

'Not at all!' James assured him. 'But you may feel a little dizzy.' He had now taken a seat in front of the equipment and was slightly to one side of it. Ed noticed that the circular red mirror was directly ahead now, pointed straight at the X. James' fingers moved across a keyboard and the constant low hum that had been in the background ever since Ed had arrived began to rise rapidly in pitch, mutating from a deep rumble to a high-pitched squeal.

'You might want to put your fingers in your ears,' Sherlock advised him and Ed had to admit the sound was starting to become uncomfortable. He noticed that both Bobby and Toby were looking extremely agitated.

'A slight side-effect that we're still trying to find a cure for,' shouted James over the screech. Ed took the advice he'd been given and jammed his index fingers into his ears, blocking out the worst of the noise.

'All right, I'm engaging the location sensor now!' bellowed James.

There was a deep crunching sound, like a heavy

goods vehicle changing gears and the red light began to mutate into a fierce white glow. Ed snatched in a breath because, as he watched, a circular opening appeared in the air directly in front of him, a shimmering, rippling band of light – and through that opening, Ed could see into another location entirely, an open space alongside a red brick wall. He was about to ask a question but then Sherlock was stepping decisively forward, one hand still on Ed's shoulder and there was no option but to go with him. They passed through the circle and for the briefest moment, Ed felt as though he was actually standing on thin air. James had been telling the truth, it didn't hurt, but it was a most unpleasant feeling, as though every atom of his being had been rubbed out with an eraser and then replaced by an identical copy. There was a long moment where emptiness seemed to drift around him and he felt as though his stomach was about to give up its contents. Then suddenly, startlingly, solid ground connected with the soles of his shoes and directly behind him there was a brief noise, as though somebody had just pulled a large zip shut. He and Sherlock were now standing in a small concrete-flagged yard, the one that James had picked out on the computer screen. It was a bright, sunny morning, perhaps a few degrees warmer than it had been in Edinburgh and somewhere nearby, birds were singing.

And then, a voice spoke right behind them. 'What the blinking flip!' it said.

FIFTEEN

The Peveril

Ed turned his head in surprise and saw that a man was standing in the yard, just behind them. He was holding a broom and must have been sweeping the yard as they arrived. He was a tubby, middle-aged fellow, with sandy-coloured hair and a bulbous nose. He was staring at Ed and Sherlock, his mouth hanging open, as though he'd never seen anything so amazing in his entire life. Ed thought about it and realised that he and Sherlock must have appeared to step out of thin air, right in front of him.

The man made a couple of unsuccessful attempts to speak again before he managed to splutter out a single sentence. 'Where the… where the hell did you two come from?' he choked.

'Umm… Edinburgh?' said Ed, trying to be helpful.

'But you… you just…' Now the man's gaze focused warily on Sherlock, taking in his weirdly pale, makeup-plastered features, the huge black hat, his dark glasses and the sheer intimidating height of him. 'Are you… are you all right?' murmured the man.

'I'm fine and dandy, thank you,' said Sherlock. 'Thank you for asking.'

'Only you look…' The man's voice trailed away. He was either unsure or unwilling to continue. 'You're not from round 'ere,' he added at last.

'No, as my young companion just stated, we're from Edinburgh. I'm sure you're familiar with Scotland's capital city? Am I to take it that I am speaking to the proprietor of this fine establishment?'

'You what?' muttered the man.

'I think he means, "Are you the landlord of the pub?"' suggested Ed.

'Oh! Er… yeah. Yeah, I am.' The man was still staring at Sherlock as though thinking about making a run for it. 'We're not open yet,' he added. 'If it's money you're after, I've already dropped off last night's takings at the bank.'

Sherlock looked outraged. 'We're not after money,' he said. 'Do we look like a pair of villains?'

The man left the question unanswered but the look on his face said that yes, they really did.

'We… we come in peace,' offered Ed and felt rather stupid for saying that.

There was a short silence and then the man said.

'I don't understand. One minute I was on my own, brushing the yard and the next minute… you were just… *there*.'

'Well, we took the fast train,' said Sherlock, as though this explained everything. 'Now, please be reassured, we're not here to rob you or harm you in any way. But I would like to ask you a few questions, if you wouldn't mind.'

The man seemed to consider this for a few moments. 'I don't want any trouble,' he said. 'Please, I'm not a well man.' He tapped his chest. 'My heart. I'm not supposed to get over-excited.'

'There's absolutely no need for concern, I can assure you.' Sherlock tried what he probably thought was an encouraging smile but on his pale, makeup-caked features it looked downright creepy, mainly because his teeth were completely black. 'Perhaps we might venture inside your delightful premises,' he suggested. 'We'll surely be more comfortable there.'

'Um… all right. Whatever you say.' The landlord propped his broom against a wall and turned towards the half-open back door. 'This way,' he said and with evident reluctance, led them inside.

It was like stepping back in time, Ed thought. The interior of the pub was a jumble of leaded glass panels and heavy wooden fittings, antique fireplaces and cast iron tables. Ed didn't know anything about pubs but he got the distinct impression that this place hadn't changed its look in a very long time.

The landlord indicated a table in one corner and invited his two visitors to sit down. Ed took one chair and Sherlock lowered himself gingerly onto another, but clearly the cast iron legs of this chair were made of sterner stuff than the one he'd tried in Starbucks. The landlord stood looking at them uncertainly. 'Can I offer you gentlemen a… drink?' he asked nervously.

'Nothing for me, thank you,' said Sherlock.

Ed slipped a hand into his pocket and pulled out a can of lemonade. 'I brought my own,' he said and set it down on the table.

'I think I'll get something,' said the landlord. He slipped in behind the bar and poured himself a large glass of amber liquid. Then he came out, sat in the vacant seat and took a large gulp from the glass. Ed noticed that the man's hand was shaking slightly as he drank.

'Isn't it a little early for that?' murmured Sherlock.

'Sorry, I had quite a shock when you two just…' He waved a hand, as though unsure of how to describe it. 'You… said something about questions?'

'Yes,' said Sherlock. 'First of all, I want you to have a good look at my young companion here. Does he seem familiar to you?'

The landlord stared blankly at Ed for a moment. 'No,' he said. 'Never seen him before in my life. Who is he?'

'That's just the problem. He doesn't know.'

'Ah.' The landlord took another gulp of his drink. 'I can see that would be awkward.'

'You're familiar, no doubt, with amnesia?' continued Sherlock.

'I've seen it now and then,' said the landlord. 'In films and that.'

'Well, let me assure you, this is no film. This young man is actually suffering from the condition. And I've been sent here to try and find out a bit more about him.'

'Sent from where?' asked the landlord.

'From Edinburgh,' said Sherlock, sounding slightly exasperated.

'I've been there a few times,' announced the landlord. 'Never saw anybody like you, though.'

'Oh, there's a huge family of us,' Sherlock assured him. 'We're all...' He thought for a moment. '...basketball players,' he added, clearly remembering something that Ed had said to him earlier. 'All right, may I enquire if you have seen a certain man in here?'

'What man?' asked the landlord. 'We get a lot of 'em.'

Sherlock glanced at Ed. 'Give him the description,' he suggested.

'Description?'

'Of the man you saw. You know, in your vision.'

'Oh, OK. Well he's fairly average-sized and...'

'Just a minute,' said the landlord, lifting a hand. 'Sorry. Did I 'ear that right? Did he just say "in your vision?"'

Ed nodded. 'Yes,' he said. 'I saw a man coming into this pub. He was about average size with sort of scruffy hair over his collar. And he was wearing a black leather jacket, blue jeans and white trainers.'

The landlord looked insulted. 'What about his face?' he asked. 'The colour of his eyes, whether he had a beard or not...'

'I only saw him from the back,' said Ed.

'Oh.' The landlord drained the last of his drink and sat there, looking at the empty glass as though considering topping it up again. 'That could be any one of hundreds of men that come in here,' he said. 'Probably thousands over a year.'

'He may have brought you a flyer featuring a picture of a dog,' suggested Sherlock. A border collie.' Sherlock waved a huge gloved hand at Ed. 'Show him,' he said.

Ed rooted though his pockets until he found the folded A4 sheet. He opened it up and slid it across the table. As soon as the landlord saw it, his expression changed dramatically.

'That means something to you, doesn't it?' Sherlock prompted him.

'Yes, it does. It's quite strange, really, only happened a week ago. A chap came in here with one of these flyers and asked me if he could put it on the community noticeboard over there.' He pointed to a cork pin board on the far side of the room that was filled with a jumble of flyers, adverts and notes. 'Of course, I said yeah, no problem.'

'Was it the man the boy described?'

'No, this was a respectable-looking chap. One of my regulars, actually, though I don't know his name. He usually stops in for a swift half on his way home from work, but he didn't bother with a drink that day. He went straight over, pinned the flyer to the board and then left.'

'He works locally then?'

'Somewhere close by, I reckon. Always very smartly dressed, wears a suit and a tie, carries a briefcase. And once or twice…'

'Yes?'

'I've noticed that he has the case handcuffed to his wrist, as though there's something valuable in it. I don't like to ask questions, mind. I think that's one of the reasons he comes in here. He seems the quiet sort.'

'A week ago, you say. You've seen him since?'

'No, I haven't, now I come to think of it. Which is odd, because like I said, he generally drops in three or four times a week. Always has just the one drink though. Careful sort of bloke. Keeps himself to himself.'

Sherlock scanned the board hopefully. 'I can't see the flyer,' he said.

'No. That's the funny thing and it's really why I remember it. Two minutes after the first chap left, another fellow arrived…' He looked at Ed. '… somebody more like the bloke you was describing, you know, scruffy type and… yeah, I think he *was* wearing a leather jacket. Big staring eyes, he had. He went straight over to the board, ripped down the flyer, shoved it in his pocket and walked out again. I thought maybe somebody was offering a reward, you know, maybe that's why he was so interested in it. He didn't stop to talk or have a drink or nothing. He just walked right out.'

Sherlock considered for a moment. 'So you did see *his* face?'

The landlord frowned. 'Yeah, just for a moment or so. It struck me then that there was something odd about him. Like I said, he had these big eyes but there was something else about him and I can't really remember what it was…' He stared into his empty glass as though seeking inspiration. 'It was something…' Then his expression changed. 'Oh yeah, that was it.' He looked up at Sherlock. 'He had no eyebrows.'

Ed looked at Sherlock, puzzled by this latest piece of information.

'That sounds weird,' he said.

Sherlock shrugged his massive metal shoulders. 'Not really,' he said. 'Quite startling to look at, I grant you, but more common than you might suppose. He was probably suffering from *Alopecia Areata*.'

'What's that?' asked Ed.

'It's an auto-immune deficiency. Hair loss is usually restricted to small patches on the head, but in severe conditions, *all* hair is lost. Severe alopecia is often linked to people who have a thyroid condition.' He looked at the landlord again. 'I believe you said something about big staring eyes. Do you mean that they were prominent… bulging, perhaps?'

The landlord considered for a moment. 'Well, yeah, first thing I noticed about him. But… alopecia don't make sense, surely? I mean, if it's severe enough to make him lose his eyebrows, wouldn't he be bald on top as well?'

Sherlock smiled. 'He may have been wearing a wig,' he said. 'Some people can be sensitive about their looks and disguise it that way. I believe that they also make false eyebrows for such sufferers, but I would doubt that many would be bothered to apply them every day. Hence the lack of any.' He glanced at Ed. 'My hunch is that we're looking for a wig-wearing alopecia sufferer with a thyroid condition,' he said.

The landlord gave a snort of amusement. 'Proper little Sherlock, aren't you?' he observed.

Sherlock looked disappointed. 'Is it that obvious?' he murmured. 'I was hoping the disguise was better than that.' He reached up a hand and lifted the broad brimmed hat he was wearing, revealing the metal deerstalker beneath it.

The landlord's eyes bulged and for a moment it looked as though *he* was the one suffering from a thyroid condition. 'I think I will have that other drink,' he murmured and got up from the table. Sherlock replaced the hat.

'So you have no idea where this fellow was headed?' he asked.

The landlord was at the bar now, refilling his glass. 'None at all. He came in the front door and went straight out again. Could have been going anywhere.' He paused for a moment and shook his head. 'I'm sorry,' he said. 'That hat...the one you're wearing under the *other* one. It... it looks like metal.'

'Bronze,' said Sherlock, matter-of-factly.

'I see.' The landlord came back to the table and sat down again. 'I hope you don't mind me asking, but why would anyone wear a metal hat?'

'It's for protection,' said Ed, hastily. 'In case... somebody drops something heavy onto his head.'

'Right. And that... that's something that could happen, is it?'

'You can never be too careful,' Sherlock told him. 'There's a lot of building work going on in this area. It would only take one workman to drop his hammer and that could be the end of me.'

'Right. And... the other hat? The one that goes over the metal one.'

'Well, one doesn't want to give an open invitation,' explained Sherlock. 'A workman up on some scaffolding could look down, see the metal hat and think of it as a challenge. He might think to himself, "let's see how effective *that* is." And then he'd just let go of his hammer. Which would be both dangerous and profoundly irritating.'

The landlord took a generous swallow of his drink. 'Makes sense I suppose,' he murmured, but Ed could see that he was barely managing to stop himself from running out of the pub, screaming for help. 'So, Mr... I'm sorry, I don't think I caught your name.'

'I don't think I threw it. But the name's Holmes.'

The landlord stared at him in evident dismay. 'As in... Sherlock Holmes?' he murmured.

Sherlock gave an unconvincing laugh. 'No, no, of course not! It's er... William Holmes! But you can call me Bill.'

'Right. Well... Bill. And...?' He glanced at Ed questioningly.

'Ed Fest,' said Ed.

'And Ed... Fest. Unless there's anything else I can help you with, I really should be getting ready to open up. Time's moving on.'

'Indeed it is.' Sherlock reached into his waistcoat pocket and pulled out a black metal watch on a black metal chain. The landlord looked at it and then drained the rest of his glass.

'Well, if you'll excuse me,' he said. 'I'll be...'

He broke off in alarm as Sherlock suddenly slapped himself on the forehead with a groan of despair. 'I'm a blithering idiot,' he cried.

SIXTEEN

The Phone Call

Ed looked at him, alarmed. 'What's the matter?' he asked.

'Give me that flyer,' said the detective. 'I have been as blind as a mole, but it is better to learn wisdom than never to learn it at all.'

'I don't understand!'

'It never even occurred to me before but of course, this is the modern world, somebody... most likely you... will almost certainly have posted this image on social media.'

'Do you think so?'

'I'd bet money on it. I don't know why it didn't occur to me to check before. Personally, I blame Starbucks!'

'Why them?'

'Didn't I tell you the mood in that place wasn't

conducive to the thought processes? Oh, for a quiet study and my violin!' He gestured at his surroundings. 'This place at least has the right kind of atmosphere.' He glanced at the landlord. 'Congratulations on that, by the way. This pub is so much better than Starbucks. You might even consider that as an advertising slogan.' He looked back at Ed. 'As if you'd confine yourself to sticking handbills on notice boards. How old fashioned would that be?' He removed his sunglasses, studied the flyer for a moment and then blinked, making a sound like a camera shutter opening and closing. He reached a hand into his coat and tapped the pipe, lifting the big hat from his head a second time. The curved screen descended from the brim of the deerstalker, across his eyes, and he stared fixedly at it, tapping the pipe a couple more times as he did so. Then his mouth curved into a black-toothed grin. 'Got it,' he said. 'And this time, I can actually read the phone number… it begins with 0161, so that means it's local!' He looked at Ed and said the number aloud. 'Does that ring any bells?' he asked.

'It does seem kind of… familiar,' said Ed.

'It should do. It's almost certainly your home phone.' He took out his mobile and punched in the digits. 'I'll put it on speaker,' he said. 'Who knows, if it *is* your home phone, we could actually have this case solved in the next five minutes.' He tapped again and the screen slid silently back into his hat.

There was a brief silence and then the phone began

to ring. While they waited, Ed studied the landlord. He was staring across the table, open-mouthed once again. He was probably wondering what kind of person kept a perspex screen in the brim of his metal hat. And what kind of person had metal eyes that could double as a camera.

'This is a lovely pub,' said Ed, trying to keep him sweet.

'Better than Starbucks,' murmured the landlord. 'Look, where have you two *really* come from?'

'We keep telling you. Edinburgh!'

The landlord smirked. 'I mean, which *planet*,' he murmured. 'Go on, you can tell me. I won't say nothing to anyone else.'

Ed opened his mouth to protest but just at the moment, the telephone call was answered. 'Yes?' asked a voice.

'Hello,' said Sherlock. 'I'm phoning regarding your lost dog, Lucky.'

There was a long silence. Then the voice said, 'Who is this?' and Ed noticed that whoever was speaking had a rather posh-sounding voice.

'More to the point, who is *this*?' countered Sherlock.

Another silence. 'What has that to do with you?'

'Well, I saw the poster advertising the missing dog and listing this phone number. So I called you. I have somebody with me who is also interested. The dog's owner, a young boy.'

'You have the boy?' Suddenly, the man on the other end of the line seemed very interested. For the first time,

Ed registered that there was something oddly familiar about the voice. But he was pretty sure it didn't belong to his father. 'Where is he?'

'He's with me,' said Sherlock. 'He's sitting right beside me at an address in Manchester.'

'Well now, you listen to me,' said the voice. 'I'm not some idiot who you can take liberties with. You will bring him to me, do you understand? It's not too late to make this work, but I need to make sure it really is him.'

Sherlock frowned. Ed could see that he was trying to work something out. 'And… what about the dog?'

'We have the dog with us and we also have the boy's father. Both of them are safe for the moment. But time is running out, my friend. If the boy wants to see his father alive, you'll get him to me quickly. And he'll bring the ransom with him. Otherwise, all bets are off.'

Sherlock glanced at Ed and raised his eyebrows. Ed had heard the man's words but didn't know what to make of them. *If he wanted to see his father alive? Ransom?* What was that supposed to mean?

Sherlock returned his attention to the phone. 'All right, we'll come. Give me the address,' he said.

'No, we'll meet in a safe place. Come to the Hulme Hippodrome at…' Another pause. Ed pictured the man looking at his watch. '… at eleven o' clock. You'll find that one of the side doors will open easily. Go into the building and wait for me to make myself known to you.'

'Very well. But I need a name.'

'What?'

'I need to call you something.'

'Don't be ridiculous. You think I'm stupid enough to tell you my name?'

'It doesn't have to be real. For instance, you can call me Bill. But I refuse to talk to anyone unless I can call them something.'

Another silence as though the man was debating the wisdom of the idea. Finally, he said, 'OK. You can call me Myles.'

'Very well, Myles, I don't suppose you have the postcode for…?'

'Listen to me. Don't try any funny business. Do you understand? If I see anyone else with you… police, back-up men, anyone other than just the two of you, the boy can say goodbye to his father *and* his flea-bitten dog. He fooled me once, but he isn't going to get another chance. This is his last opportunity to make good. Bring me the diamonds. If you don't have them when you arrive, it will not go well with his father. I only need to make one phone call and the man is dead. It's as simple as that.'

'The… diamonds,' murmured Sherlock. 'What diamonds?'

'You know what diamonds. *He* knows what diamonds! If he's not mentioned them to you, then just ask him. He was supposed to bring them to me yesterday, but instead, he decided to make a run for it.'

'Where was this?'

'You ask too many questions, my friend.'

'I'm simply trying to establish a few facts. Where did you last see the boy? What harm can it do you to tell me that much?'

A sigh. 'At Piccadilly Station. He was jumping on a train.'

'I see. And… I expect you must know the boy's name?'

'Of course I know his name! What do you take me for, an amateur?'

'You don't understand. The boy is suffering from amnesia.'

'Oh yes? And I'm St Francis of Assisi. Now, just bring him along to the meeting place and don't be late.'

'And his name? What's his name?'

'Enough! I'm getting a little tired of all these questions. All you need to know is that his father is alive and well for the moment, but I am very close to changing that situation. Do you understand? Don't push me any more.'

'And how do I know you're telling the truth? I need proof.'

'I'm afraid you're going to have to take my word for it, old boy. Eleven o'clock, *Bill*. Don't be late.' With that, the man rang off. Ed and Sherlock sat there looking at each other in stunned surprise. There was a very long silence.

'Well, I'll confess I didn't expect that,' said Sherlock, at last.

Ed didn't know what to say. 'Somebody has kidnapped my dad?' he muttered. 'And my dog?'

'It would appear so.'

'Somebody... posh?'

'A Londoner, judging by the accent. And clearly a man who will stop at nothing to obtain whatever he needs.' Sherlock got up from his seat and began to pace about, a look of intense concentration on his face. Ed was horribly aware of the landlord listening in on everything that was being said, his mouth still hanging open like a stranded fish.

'Let's try and put together everything we know and what we can easily guess at,' suggested Sherlock. 'Usually I never guess. It is a shocking habit – destructive to the logical faculty... but at the moment, I have little other choice. I'm going to suggest this as the sequence of events.' He cleared his throat. 'This Myles and his men... I'm assuming he wasn't working alone, we know of at least one other member of his gang...'

'We do?' asked Ed.

'Of course. The scruffy fellow who took the flyer from the pub. I'm guessing that the other man, the smartly-dressed one, was your father.'

'How do you know the man in the pub wasn't the man on the phone?' asked Ed.

Sherlock shook his head. 'Somebody like Myles would never do his own donkeywork. He will have his own Gormleys to do that for him. Now, shush a moment!' He refocused himself. 'The gang must have had their eyes on your father as a potential target, perhaps for some time. We don't know what your father does for a living, but I'm willing to bet it has something to do with diamonds – high quality diamonds. The detail about the handcuffs suggests that he's used to carrying things of high value in his briefcase. These villains needed to create an opening for themselves, so I believe they took your dog, knowing that sooner or later you would put up a flyer asking for people to be on the lookout for him. They made sure that the flyer would be seen by as few people as possible, by getting somebody to take them down just as soon as they were posted .'

'The scruffy man in the pub!' cried Ed.

'Exactly. I would suggest that they then phoned you, saying they had Lucky and invited you to go somewhere to collect him. You set out to meet them, completely unsuspicious of their motives, because they had merely answered your own enquiry. But while you were gone, Myles' accomplices visited your home and abducted your father.'

'You can't know that!' protested Ed.

'I don't, but it's an educated guess. Your father… and I'm convinced that's who he is, hasn't been back here for his usual drink in over a week. You'll note when we spoke to Myles there was no mention of your mother, so I'm going to assume that you and your father live alone together. He's probably a divorcee or… forgive me for suggesting this, a widower.'

'You don't think I have a mum?'

'No. Or at least, if you still do, she doesn't live with you and your father. At any rate, when you reached the meeting place you were met by this Myles, who told you that he had taken your father captive and that if you wanted him to be released, safe and well, you would first have to retrieve some diamonds as a ransom... perhaps they were hidden in your home, perhaps you had to get them from wherever your father worked...' He broke off, looking thoughtful. 'The little piece of paper,' he said. 'The one you had in your pocket. Have you got it?'

'Er... yeah.' Ed rooted in his pockets until he found it. He handed it to Sherlock and the detective unfolded it to reveal the six figures. 'This is obviously the combination for a safe,' he said. The villains must have obtained it from your father and handed it to you, so you could collect the diamonds. I really do think this is your birthdate, something your father would easily remember as a combination. At any rate, you collected the diamonds, as instructed, and set out to meet your father's abductors, but then something happened... and this is the area where I cannot be sure of anything, but for some reason, instead of delivering the ransom, as planned, you ran away. I would suggest you were being chased by Myles and his gang, how else did they know you'd jumped on a train? Perhaps you arrived at the station just as it was leaving for Edinburgh and you threw yourself on board. After that… well, we pretty much know the rest.'

'But why do it that way round?' asked the landlord unexpectedly, and Sherlock turned to glare at him. 'Sorry, I don't mean to interrupt, but seriously, why not just kidnap the boy and tell the *father* to bring the diamonds?'

Sherlock frowned. 'Because, that's what everyone would expect them to do. But I would suggest that if the boy's father works in the diamond industry, he's doubtless been trained for such an eventuality. He would have gone straight to the police, which is, of course, the correct thing to do in these circumstances. But a young boy, now… he wouldn't have a clue about how to handle the situation. He'd be so much easier to manipulate. He'd be scared, anxious, he'd do everything he was told in order to save his father. Much easier to get the combination of a safe, for instance, from the father and have the boy collect the diamonds.' Sherlock studied Ed for a few moments. 'Our friend Myles is pretty convinced that you had them at the station,' he said. 'So, if that's the case, what happened to them?'

Ed shrugged his shoulders. 'I've no idea,' he said.

Sherlock took out his mobile phone and rang another number. It was answered straight away and he spoke quickly and directly. 'James,' he said. 'I have two tasks for you. Firstly, I want you to find the co-ordinates for something called The Hulme Hippodrome in

Manchester and I want you to find me a safe place to set down there as soon as possible. Open an entry portal in the same position as before, in the back yard of the pub. I also need you to run a check on this phone number…' He pressed a button on the mobile and there was a beeping sound. '… find which address that belongs to and create a way to get us there quickly, but wait until I contact you before setting the co-ordinates. Got that? Good. I'll talk to you soon.' He signed off and slipped the phone into his pocket. 'Now,' he said. 'There's the little matter of those diamonds.' He looked intently at Ed. 'Myles says you had them with you at the station. Unless you dropped them or mislaid them, the chances are you still have them on you.'

Ed spread his arms in a gesture of helplessness. 'But you already looked at everything,' he protested.

'Indeed I did. Which means there's only one place they can possibly be.' He leant forward and reached out to Ed's neck. He found the length of cord around his neck and lifted it to release the large metal whistle. He weighed it in his hand for a moment, his expression thoughtful; then he set the whistle down on the table top and with a swift movement, brought his fist down on it, popping it neatly open.

Inside it was a tiny plastic bag, which seemed to shimmer and glitter with myriad reflections of light.

'Not a dog whistle at all,' observed Sherlock. 'Just an ordinary one, stuffed with diamonds. Which accounts for the strange sound it makes when you blow into it. And for the fact that I thought it surprisingly heavy when I first examined it.' He lifted the bag of gems and brought it up to his gaze. 'Hmm. And not just ordinary diamonds but pale pink fancies – incredibly rare, and extremely valuable, despite their modest size. This tiny pack could be worth more than a million pounds in today's money.'

Ed felt his jaw drop open. He sat there, realising that he now made a perfect duo with the landlord. 'I… I didn't even know I *had* them,' he murmured.

'Of course you didn't. You have amnesia! But you must have chosen to hide them in this.' He stuffed the package back into the hollow whistle and clipped the metal side shut over it. 'See, it pops back on securely. Clearly this is a hiding place you've used before for other small items – and somewhere that nobody would ever think of looking. Well chosen!' He went to hand the whistle back to Ed but the boy waved it away.

'Would you mind keeping it for me?' he asked. 'I might lose it.'

Sherlock nodded and tucked the whistle into his waistcoat pocket. He replaced his dark glasses, then took out his watch and consulted it. 'We should think about getting to the Hippodrome,' he announced. 'Myles said eleven o'clock but I've always preferred to be ahead of schedule.' He looked apologetically at the landlord. 'I'm sorry you've had to witness all this,' he said. 'I would have much preferred to keep everything more discreet but, alas, that was not to be.'

The landlord nodded feebly. 'That's OK,' he mumbled. 'It's been an education.'

'I'm going to have to trouble you for the use of your back yard one more time and then we'll be out from under your feet.'

'No problem,' said the landlord.

'Of course, I will now have to kill you.'

'What?' The landlord looked horrified.

Sherlock bared his black teeth. 'Only joking,' he said. 'You may of course, report the events you've witnessed today to anybody you like, though I would humbly suggest that you'd do better to keep them to yourself. People are liable to think that you've let your imagination run away with you if you start talking about...'

'Aliens,' muttered the landlord.

'Oh, no, sir, we're not aliens,' Sherlock assured him. 'Ed here is a perfectly ordinary boy with amnesia and I'm a bronze statue that comes to life for one day a year. But as it happens, a statue friend of mine has invented an apparatus that can take us anywhere in the world, instantly, and that's how we come to be here in your charming pub. May I just congratulate you on having one of the best preserved interiors I've ever witnessed?'

'Er... thanks,' grunted the landlord.

'Well...' Sherlock ushered Ed to stand up. 'Thank you so much for your help. We'll be going now.'

'Goodbye,' said the landlord, with surprising calmness, but as Ed and Sherlock headed for the back door, he was up out of his seat and scurrying back to the bar, empty glass in hand.

'I hope we haven't completely deranged him,' whispered Sherlock. He opened the back door and stepped out into the yard.

SEVENTEEN

The Hippodrome

The portal was waiting for them out in the yard, hanging a few inches above the stone flags, shimmering and rippling on the empty air and making that high-pitched screeching sound. Through the opening, Ed could see another location. On a short stretch of road that ran beside some park railings, there was a huge three-storey building of red brick. It looked totally anonymous and not what he'd been expecting at all. The words 'Hulme Hippodrome' had made him imagine a huge glitzy place but this looked like any old deserted warehouse.

Sherlock placed a hand on his shoulder. 'Ready?' he asked.

Ed nodded, so Sherlock took a breath and stepped forward. Once again there was that curious melting sensation, the feeling that all of Ed's atoms were being erased and replaced. He had the same sensation of standing on the air before tarmac appeared beneath the soles of his shoes and there was that brief ripping sound from just behind him. This time he remembered to look around quickly, but as far as he could see there was nobody here to observe their arrival. The area looked deserted.

'Come on,' said Sherlock and they walked along the street towards what must have been the building's boarded-up entrance, which was plastered with layers of graffiti. Sherlock examined the entrance but found no easy way in.

'The man on the phone said something about a door round the side,' Ed reminded him. He led the way along the front and around the corner, where a narrow alley ran up the side of the theatre. They soon found another boarded-up, slogan-scrawled entrance, but when they examined it closer they found that the board was secured only at one corner and could be easily swung aside. They stepped into a gloomy entranceway and hesitated for a moment before Sherlock pulled out his mobile phone and clicked a torch app, which sent a powerful beam of light ahead of them.

They passed through another doorway and found themselves in the building's huge interior. They paused and Sherlock sent the beam of light in all directions, giving them some idea of the scale of the place.

'Wow,' muttered Ed. The humble exterior had given no clue to the sheer majesty that lay within. It was a massive old theatre, with a stage framed by a gigantic decorative arch. In front of the stage was an open space.

'That must be where the pipe organ was located,' said Sherlock knowingly. He sent the torch beam around in a slow circle, revealing rows and rows of red velvet seats, once luxurious, but now liberally spotted with dollops of white bird droppings. As if to accentuate the point there was a brief flutter of wings and a pigeon flapped frantically away from the torch beam and off into the gloom.

Sherlock reached into a pocket and took out his pipe. There was a soft humming sound as the perspex visor slid down from his hat brim and then he was reading aloud to Ed, snippets from the article he could see onscreen. 'The Hulme Hippodrome. Opened in 1901, now a grade II listed building. Not that you'd guess from the state of it! All the greats have performed here, over the years. Dame Nellie Melba. Laurel and Hardy. The Beatles… whoever they were. It became a bingo hall in the 1970's and finally closed down in the 1980's. There are vague plans to try and restore it to its former glory but they'd need twenty million pounds to do that and it seems unlikely they'll raise it.' Sherlock shook his head. 'What a shame.'

'Why did Myles tell us to meet him here?' murmured Ed apprehensively.

'I presume because he wanted somewhere where we won't be disturbed. It's all too evident that nobody ever comes here.'

'So what are we going to do when he turns up?'

'We'll find out what he knows. After that, I'm not sure. Anyway, we won't have to wait long.'

'But he said eleven o'clock.'

'He did, but if he's any good at his job, he'll have come much earlier than that. He'll want to stake the place out, make sure we haven't brought anyone else with us. In fact, I'd be willing to bet that he's already here somewhere, skulking in the shadows...'

'You're a clever chap,' said a suave voice from somewhere in the darkness and then powerful stage lights snapped on, making them both blink. As Ed's eyes focused, he became aware of a man strolling out onto the stage from his hiding place in the wings; a stocky fellow with neatly cut grey hair and intense blue eyes. He was wearing a suede coat with a sheepskin collar and Ed noticed that his rather fancy shoes had been polished until they shone like black mirrors. Just behind him trailed another man, tall and skinny, wearing a greasy-looking black leather jacket. He had long, scruffy hair that seemed somehow too big for his head and his oddly bulging eyes looked all the stranger because there were no eyebrows above them.

'You!' hissed Ed and in that instant it all came flooding back to him in a rush of sight and sound.

For a moment he was back, walking nervously along a Manchester street with the skinny, goggle-eyed man, the two of them turning left and right along a maze of back streets until they found themselves standing outside the *Peveril of the Peak*. 'Wait 'ere a minute,'

Skinny, had said, speaking with a local accent. 'The guy who has your dog is inside. I'll bring him out here to have a quick talk with you.'

And he had stepped through the door of the pub, which swung shut behind him. Ed stood there, waiting impatiently to hear about Lucky. It had been almost a week now and the boy was frantic for news of his much-loved pet. He had nearly given up hope when he'd received the phone call yesterday afternoon, a Friday, a man's voice he didn't recognise telling him that Lucky had been found. There was no mistake, the man said, because the dog's name was engraved on a little metal tag on his collar. The man on the phone had a local accent and he told the boy to meet him outside Piccadilly Station the following day, Saturday. The boy said that he would need to check with his dad when he got back from work, but the man said, 'No, why bother him? I'm sure he's busy enough,' and the boy had to admit that yes, Dad *was* busy, he always worked Saturdays and made no exceptions, so *he* wouldn't be able to accompany Ed into Manchester.

After a bit of frantic thinking, he decided to ask a friend to go with him instead, a boy called Luke and that was all set up until Luke phoned half an hour before the two of them were due to set off, saying he'd come down with a stinking cold and couldn't go with him.

He knew it was wrong, but Dad had already left for work and Ed was desperate to get Lucky back, so against all his better judgement he went by himself to Piccadilly Station and now here he was, standing outside the pub, waiting for Skinny to return…

And finally, finally, the door opened again and Skinny emerged with another man, the one who called himself Myles and Ed felt a rush of excitement, because Myles had Lucky with him. He was walking him on a lead and the man was smiling at him. But the boy noticed that the smile did not extend to his eyes and he began to feel afraid because there was something about Myles, something dangerous in the steely glint of those blue eyes and the mocking twist of his smile. The boy stepped impulsively forward to claim Lucky but Myles lifted a hand to stop him in his tracks. And then he explained the situation calmly and quietly, glancing from side to side every so often to ensure that he wasn't being overheard by anyone passing by.

'Listen carefully to me, boy. We have your father. Do you understand? We took him on his way to work this morning and if you want him back alive, you are going to have to do a little favour for me.' The man reached into the pocket of his suede coat and withdrew a slip of paper which he pressed into the boy's hand. Ed looked at it in bewilderment. He noted that there was a code written on it. He recognised his father's distinctive writing and also his own date of birth.

1-6-0-7-0-2.

'That is the combination of the safe in your father's study,' explained Myles. 'You are to go straight home, open the safe and take out the small packet of pink diamonds stored on the bottom shelf. Then you will bring them to me.' He leaned closer and Ed could smell the sour, garlicky stink of his breath. 'Don't even think about going to the police or to a friend or relative. You will tell nobody about this. And I do mean *nobody*. You will come to Piccadilly Station – the same place you met my friend here earlier. You will waste no time over this, do you understand? As soon as you have the diamonds, you will bring them to the station.'

The boy nodded, dumbly, too shocked to speak.

'Good. I want you to remember that my friend here will be watching you every step of the way. If he sees anything wrong, any other person with you or following you, he will tell me, and you will never see your father again. Do you believe me?'

Ed nodded a second time. He was afraid of Myles because he could somehow tell that the man had done terrible things; that he was capable of just about anything. But now Myles did something unexpected. He pressed the dog lead into the boy's hand.

'Here's your dog,' he said. 'I'm giving him to you as a gesture of good faith. But it means that you owe me. So do not delay. Go home, get the diamonds, bring them to the station. When I have them, you will wait twenty-four hours and you will tell nobody what has happened. Then I will contact you and tell you where your father is being held. You'll be able to go and get him. Do you understand what you have to do?'

Ed nodded. He was afraid to even look the man in the eyes.

'Say it!'

'I understand.'

'Good. Off you go then. And don't waste any time. Remember, we will be watching you.'

The boy turned and walked away, taking Lucky with him…

And suddenly, everything receded and he was back, back in the deserted theatre, the lights on the stage blazing into his eyes and he gave a gasp and almost fell. Sherlock put out a gloved hand to steady him. 'Are you all right?' he asked.

Ed nodded. 'I remember,' he gasped. He pointed to the stage. 'That man made me get the diamonds. He has my father. You were right about the combination. It was for the safe at home.'

Sherlock shook his head in evident disgust and looked up at Myles. 'You, sir, are a contemptible coward,' he said. 'Using a young boy in such a craven fashion. You should be ashamed of yourself.'

Myles laughed at this but even so, he seemed puzzled. 'And who are you exactly?' he hissed. 'More to the point, *what* are you? You look like a freak. You don't even look human.'

'I'm not,' Sherlock assured him. 'And when I

see some examples of that race, I'm very glad to be different.'

The two men on the stage exchanged baffled looks. Then Myles turned back to look at Sherlock. 'Well, whatever you are, I didn't come here to talk,' he said. 'Do you have the diamonds?'

'Yes indeed,' said Sherlock. 'Thank you very much.'

Myles' eyes narrowed. 'So... hadn't you better hand them over?'

'If I do that,' murmured Sherlock, 'how do I know you'll honour your part of the agreement and let the boy's father go free?'

'You *don't* know that. I'm afraid you're just going to have to trust me.'

Sherlock laughed softly. 'Forgive me,' he said. 'But nothing you've done so far inspires my trust.' He paused for a moment and then smiled. 'So, you're from London – that great cesspool into which all loungers and idlers are irresistibly drained. You're from Knightsbridge, judging by your accent. You're clearly knowledgeable about diamonds, so I'd say you're in the trade. I wouldn't be totally surprised if you're an associate of the boy's father. Perhaps you even work alongside him. At any rate, you found out that he had a consignment of pale pink fancies in his home and you realised the value of them. You saw an opportunity to be rich. So you devised a plan to kidnap the boy's dog.' He paused. 'Am I warm?' he asked.

Myles' jaw dropped open in amazement. 'You may be a nine foot tall freak but you're surprisingly smart,' he observed. 'Too smart for your own good, I would say. Are you police?'

'No, I'm a detective.'

Myles gestured to Skinny, who reached into his jacket and pulled out a big, automatic pistol, which he pointed at Sherlock's chest.

'You're gonna be a dead detective if you don't hand over those diamonds sharpish,' he snarled. 'I'm going to count to three…'

'Oh, save yourself the trouble,' said Sherlock. 'For one thing it's needlessly melodramatic and for another, I seriously doubt that a man of your breeding could count that high without using his fingers.' He began to walk towards the stage, pulling Ed in behind him as he did so, offering him cover from any gunfire.

Skinny's face registered irritation but Myles lifted a hand. 'He's just trying to make you angry,' he said. 'Ignore the taunts.' He pointed at Sherlock. 'That's close enough, freak.'

But Sherlock kept walking. 'I'm going to reach into my pocket now,' he said. 'I assure you, I do not have a weapon, I'm just getting the diamonds. Don't do anything foolish.' He reached a hand slowly into his waistcoat and pulled it out again, lifting the whistle by its cord so that it flashed enticingly in the stage lights.

'What's *that* supposed to be?' sneered Myles.

'I should have thought it was quite obvious that it's

a whistle,' said Sherlock. 'The diamonds are hidden inside it. Actually, I wanted to have a word with you about them,' he added, moving closer still, until he was standing right at the edge of the stage.

'What about them?' snapped Myles, sounding suspicious.

'I don't quite know how to break this to you. You see, I had the opportunity to examine them in some detail, before we set off. Now, you can't blame the boy for this, he only did what you told him to do, he obeyed your commands to the letter...'

'What are you blathering about?' bellowed Myles.

'I'm afraid these diamonds are fakes. Oh, very good ones, they'd fool anyone who wasn't an expert, but they didn't fool me for an instant.'

'He's lying,' said Skinny.

'Of course he is,' agreed Myles.

'I assure you I'm not. You see, the best way to tell is to hold them up to the light...' Sherlock set the whistle down on the edge of the stage. 'If you'll allow me,' he said. He brought his clenched fist down onto the whistle, popping it open. Then he picked up the tiny plastic package between a massive thumb and forefinger and raised his arm. The eyes of the two men on the stage followed the packet. 'If you look carefully, you'll see that these gems are just a little too clear to be genuine pink fancies. A true fancy has a dull, almost opaque quality...'

The two men moved warily closer, Skinny keeping

the gun trained on Sherlock's chest. Ed cowered behind the detective, all too aware that this could go horribly wrong.

'Just hand them over,' insisted Myles.

'Gladly. A man of your evident experience will be able to see at a glance that they're not the real thing.' Sherlock lowered his arm somewhat and held the package tantalisingly out towards Skinny, who took the last few steps to the edge of the stage. 'Now, as I said, you mustn't blame the boy and you know what? I wouldn't be at all surprised if his father didn't know about it either. As I said, these are exceptionally good fakes...'

'Stop talking!' Skinny warned him, but Sherlock kept right on.

'You see, I've been thinking about this. How would you even know what the boy's father did for a living unless you were an inside man at the company he works for? Somebody who knew he'd been given the diamonds for safe keeping. But think about this. What if others at the company suspected that there was a mole working there? What if they gave the boy's father some fakes and *told* him they were genuine? Just to try and draw you out? I mean, he's not going to check too carefully, is he? He'd have taken their word for it. Not a very nice thing to do, I'll grant you, but... not outside the realms of possibility.'

'For the last time,' snapped Myles. 'Hand over the diamonds or I'll tell my man to shoot you where you stand.'

'Oh, there's no need for such unpleasantness. Here, please, check them for yourself.' Sherlock went to hand the packet over to Skinny and then said, 'Oops!' and let it drop. Skinny just couldn't help himself. He made an instinctive grab for the falling gems and in that same instant, Sherlock reached up, took hold of his gun hand and gave a sharp tug. 'Watch out, Ed!' he yelled.

Everything seemed to happen in slow motion. Skinny lurched forward as though he'd been yanked by a carthorse. His wig slipped down over his eyes and he sailed into the air as Sherlock ducked under him. The gun went off and a bullet thudded into a velvet seat a few rows back. Ed was aware of the man somersaulting over him and then hurtling down onto the hard floor with a loud thud. The gun slipped from his grasp and went skittering away across the floor. Ed ran for it, snatched it up and turned back to point it at Skinny but the man lay unmoving on the wooden floor, seemingly out cold.

Now Sherlock was vaulting up over the edge of the stage and Myles was backing away, shaking his head from side to side. He reached into his coat and pulled out a pistol of his own. 'Stay back!' he roared. 'I'm warning you.'

'You're warning me what?' asked Sherlock. 'That you'll shoot me if I come any closer? I say, do your worst, you ruffian!'

Sherlock kept walking towards him. At the last moment there was the shocking sound of gunfire and Ed saw a flash of flame light up Sherlock's face, which twisted into an expression of pain. He hesitated for a moment, while Myles stood there staring up at him in disbelief.

'Ouch,' said Sherlock. 'That really *hurt*.' Then he lifted a hand and bought his clenched fist down hard on the top of Myles' head, knocking him flat.

'Sherlock, are you all right?' cried Ed.

The statue looked thoughtful and rubbed at his chest for a moment. There was a sudden clatter as the bullet dropped onto the stage. 'I do believe the villain's left a dent,' he complained. 'That'll be hard to explain away.' He stooped to ensure that Myles was unconscious and then turned to look at Ed. 'What about our other friend?' he asked. Ed kneeled and lifted off the man's wig, revealing a completely bald skull. Skinny was clearly unconscious.

'He's sorted,' said Ed.

'Excellent,' said Sherlock. 'Well, I would suggest that you put that gun down before it goes off and injures somebody. Then start looking for something we can use to tie these two villains up. There's no time to waste.'

Ed was puzzled by this remark. 'But… we've beaten them,' he cried. 'Once they're tied up, surely all we need to do is call the police?'

'Sadly, it's not going to be quite as easy as that. We need to find your father before the rest of the gang realise that something's gone wrong. Hurry, boy! The game's afoot and we need to get moving!'

EIGHTEEN

Home Sweet Home

When Myles woke up to find himself bound hand and foot with lengths of electrical flex, sitting on the stage beside a similarly bound and still unconscious Skinny, he was not a happy man. He shook his head until his senses cleared and then his blue eyes focused and shot pure venom at Ed and Sherlock, who were standing a short distance away from him.

'Untie me!' he snarled. 'I'm warning you, you'd better do as I say.'

'Oh yeah, we're really going to do that,' said Ed. 'Not.'

Myles sneered. 'You think you're in the clear now? Don't be fooled. If my people don't hear from me in the next five minutes, they have orders to execute your father.'

'Is that right?' said Sherlock. 'The next five minutes, you say? That's very specific. I mean, you don't even know how long you've been unconscious, do you? You could have been out for thirty minutes and now it's already too late.'

Myles grimaced. 'All right, I take your point. All I'm saying is, if they don't get a call from me, *very soon*, saying that I have the diamonds, they know exactly what they have to do.'

'How many of them are there?' asked Sherlock.

'Wouldn't you like to know?'

'Well, yes, that's why I asked.' Sherlock moved closer to Myles. 'However many there are, I would suggest it's time to call off the dogs,' he said.

'You think I'm going to tell them to stand down?' mocked Myles. 'You must be joking. There's nothing you can do to make me call them.'

'There's no need,' said Sherlock. He clamped a huge bronze hand over Myles' mouth and then searched his pockets. He pulled out a mobile phone and quickly scanned the contacts. 'Ah,' he said. 'This number looks familiar.' He pressed 'dial' and waited a few moments. When somebody answered with a low grunt, Sherlock spoke in a perfect impression of Myles' voice. 'It's me,' he said. 'We have the diamonds. Stand down and wait for my instructions.' Then he rang off, dropped the phone back into Myles' pocket and removed his other hand from the man's mouth.

'That was amazing,' observed Ed. 'You sounded just like him.'

'Yes, I've often considered impressionism as a second career,' said Sherlock.

'You think they fell for *that*?' laughed Myles, but somehow his manner was less confident than before.

'Oh, definitely,' said Sherlock, with a smile. 'Hook, line and sinker, I'd say, especially as it came from your phone. And I used the phrase 'stand down,' which I wouldn't have thought of if you hadn't suggested it to me. You know, it really would have been a good idea to put a security code on your phone, though I've no doubt I'd have soon worked it out.' He looked at Ed. 'Well, that's bought us a little time to think. Now, the question is, what happens next?' He thought for a moment. 'First things first. Myles must have his diamonds. After all, I did promise them to him.' He opened his hand to reveal the small packet of gems lying on his gloved palm.

'But… I thought you said they were fakes,' cried Ed.

'Oh, I *said* that, but they're actually not. No, these are genuine pink fancies. Worth a king's ransom.' He walked closer and stuffed the diamonds into the top pocket of Myles' overcoat, leaving them hanging out a little so that they wouldn't be missed. 'There you are,' he said.

Ed stared at him in disbelief. 'You're giving him the diamonds?' he cried.

'Most certainly. They're incriminating evidence. And I want to be sure that even the most incompetent policeman can't fail to notice them.' He took out his own phone and dialled a number. He waited for a moment until it was answered, then adopted the voice of an elderly man with a Manchester accent. 'Hello? Is that the police? Look, I just saw two very suspicious-looking blokes walking into the Hulme Hippodrome. Yeah, that's right. The Hippodrome. They went in through a side door and they was carrying guns. Big, dangerous-looking weapons. They looked really dodgy. Me? Just a concerned member of the public. Bye for now!' He rang off and Myles' face twisted into a mask of fury. He started to unleash a barrage of curses.

Sherlock gave him a disapproving look. 'And there I was thinking that you were a gentleman,' he told Myles. 'Please moderate your language, there's a child present.' He gestured to Ed. 'Right, come on, we need to go and get your father.'

Ed stared at Sherlock. 'But… we don't know where he is,' he said.

'Of course we do.' Sherlock smiled. 'Oh, come on, think about it for a moment. It's elementary, my dear Ed. What number do you suppose I just called on Myles' phone?'

Ed frowned. 'I've no idea,' he said.

'Well, I'll give you a little clue. It was a number I recognised. One that I phoned earlier today. Come along, you know my methods. Apply them!'

Ed thought about it. 'It must have been… the number on the flyer?' he suggested.

'Correct! And think about that number for a moment.

Can you remember what I said about the first four digits?'

'They were… 0161,' murmured Ed. 'So…'

'Go on.'

'Is it…?' A number had just come into his head; a strangely familiar number. Now that he thought about it, it was the same number that had been on the poster featuring Lucky. He recited it, and Sherlock nodded.

'That's right,' he said.

'So you think… you think my dad is… at home?'

'Seems like the perfect move to me,' he said. 'You won't remember if this is the case, but I'm guessing your house is a fairly quiet place. I think when you got away from him at the station, Myles ordered his gang to take your father back to his own house. When you think about it, it's the perfect hideaway! Being away from home, without explanation, would be more suspicious. They had no idea how long it would be until you turned up again, so they settled down to wait for information, or until you turned up. I'll be very surprised if your father isn't being held there.' He looked at Myles. 'Well?' he said. 'Am I on the right track?'

Myles sneered and turned his head away.

'That's as good as an admission,' said Sherlock. He lifted his mobile for the third time and rang the speed dial. It was answered almost instantly. 'James?' he murmured. 'Hello old chap. Look, we're on the move again. Same pick up point. You remember the number I gave you earlier? Did you manage to trace the address?

You did? Chorlton-cum-Hardy, you say?' He smiled, glanced triumphantly at Ed. 'In South Manchester. Excellent! Well, I want you to patch me through to that address but set me down a little distance away from the actual house. I need to be a bit careful with this one. I want to have a good look at the place before I go in there. Marvellous. Talk to you soon.'

He slipped the phone into his pocket and smiled down at Ed. 'I told you I had the right accent,' he said. He started to walk away but then thought for a moment and turned back towards the stage. 'You know, Myles… or whatever your *real* name is, I'm quite sure you wouldn't have revealed that. It's obvious that the game's up for you. You're going to be in prison for a long time, so the very least you could do, before we leave, is tell this boy what his real name is.'

Myles' eyes widened in anger. 'Why the hell would I do that?' he roared.

'Well, it would be a nice gesture, wouldn't it? So, can I tempt you? No?' Sherlock rolled his eyes. 'Some people,' he said. 'They're such bad losers.' He turned back to Ed. 'Come on,' he said. 'I expect your father knows what you're really called. No doubt he'll be able to tell you in person soon enough.' He walked to the edge of the stage and jumped down to the ground, his heavy frame thudding onto the wooden floor. He turned and helped Ed down.

'You!' roared Myles, straining helplessly against his bonds. 'Whoever you are, *what*ever you are, you are dead meat. You hear me? When I am out of prison, I will track you down and I will kill you!'

Sherlock studied him for a moment. 'You're *most* welcome to try,' he said. 'Though I feel I must warn you that I'm not really alive in the usual sense of the word. Enjoy prison, old boy... and while you're in there, do try and mend your wicked ways.' He looked at Ed. 'Come on,' he said.

Sherlock led the way out of the theatre and back to the exit. Pushing aside the wooden board, he and Ed emerged onto the alleyway, blinking in the bright sunshine. As they came out onto the street, Ed spotted the Anomaly portal shimmering and swirling just above the tarmac. Once again the area was deserted. As they came closer to it, Ed looked through the aperture and saw in the near distance, a white-painted cottage, framed by trees. The image struck a chord with him. He knew this place. He knew it really well.

He and Sherlock stood for a moment, looking through the portal.

'Familiar?' asked Sherlock, at last.

'Oh yes,' said Ed. 'That's my home.'

'I'm very glad to hear it. Let's see if anyone's in, shall we?' He turned his head at the sound of approaching sirens. 'Ah, here come the boys in blue,' he said. 'Good response time, too. I rather wish we could hang around to watch Myles and his friend being arrested for possession of those stolen diamonds, but... as ever, time is against us.'

He placed a bronze hand on Ed's shoulder and together they stepped through the portal.

*

They were standing in a small copse of trees that edged a quiet stretch of road. On the far side of it, Ed could see the house, a little, white-painted two-storey cottage, set a short distance away from its neighbours. It was so familiar to him that he longed to run across to the gate, open it and wander up the path to the front door. He reached into his pocket and took out the single Chubb key he had carried with him all the time he'd been away. He somehow knew that it would fit the lock on that door. He looked hopefully up at Sherlock.

'Hold your horses, old chap,' murmured the detective. 'We need to be circumspect.'

'I don't even know what that means,' whispered Ed.

'It means we can't go stampeding over there like two prize bulls in a china shop.' Sherlock reached into one of his pockets and took out what looked like a small pair of binoculars, but Ed noticed that they had a small button on the side of them. When Sherlock pressed it, the glasses lit up with an eerie glow.

'Another of James' inventions?' he murmured.

'Yes.' Sherlock lifted the glasses to his eyes and

trained them on the house. 'Dashed useful, actually. They allow me to see through solid walls and detect body heat. James doesn't really have a name for them yet, though personally, I favour "X-Ray Specs." Has a nice ring to it, don't you think?' He trained the glasses on the cottage and swung them slowly from side to side, then let out a sigh. 'This is going to be trickier than I thought,' he said. He handed the glasses to Ed. 'Have a look and see how many you can count.'

Ed lifted the glasses to his eyes. Now, incredibly, he was looking straight through the walls of the house and he could see the ghostly red shapes of people moving around in a room on the ground floor. One figure was seated on a sofa and had his hands held in front of him, as though praying. Sitting on the floor beside him was a dog-shaped blur. *Lucky*, Ed thought and felt grateful that nothing bad appeared to have happened to him. He moved the glasses left and right and saw why Sherlock wanted to be cautious. There were another three red shapes in the same room and when he tilted the glasses up to the first floor, he saw that there was another shape standing at a sink in the bathroom and a fifth lying on a bed at the back of the house, apparently reading a newspaper.

'What can we do?' he murmured. 'There's only two of us.'

Sherlock nodded. 'I'm beginning to think we might need some reinforcements,' he said. 'I generally prefer to work on my own, but sometimes one has to make an exception. At all costs, we can't allow any harm to come to the hostages.' He seemed to be thinking frantically. After a few moments he took out his phone and hit the speed dial. 'James, I'm sorry to bother you again, old boy, but we have another complication,' he murmured. 'You remember what we discussed before – the possibility of sending chosen statues to certain locations? I'm wondering if this might be the perfect time to try it out?' He paused, listened for a moment. 'Well, yes, I appreciate that, but we have to test it eventually and I'm in a bit of a tight corner here. Yes!' Another pause. 'Well, I'd say, *two* ought to be enough. Mind you, it would need to be fellows who don't mind a bit of rough stuff. I know you've devised a programme that allows you to track individuals and transport them to… Yes, of course I know it could go wrong! But this *is* rather desperate, so we'll have to cross that bridge when we get to it.'

There was another lengthy pause. Ed was aware of James' voice talking frantically at the other end of the line. 'Yes,' said Sherlock. 'Of course I'll take full responsibility.' Another pause. 'I don't know, I'll have to leave the choice to you, I'm afraid. I'm a little preoccupied. Just make sure it's two fellows who don't mind getting their hands dirty. You know, military types. Yes, send them to the same location you just sent us. Leave all the explaining to me. I know it's a tall order, but… well, see what you can do, all right? And time is of the essence, my friend, so please act quickly. Splendid.'

He rang off and looked at Ed. 'We'll just have to cool our heels for a moment while James sorts things out at his end.'

Ed, meanwhile, had lowered the binoculars and was staring intently at the house. It was the strangest thing, but as he looked at it, memories were beginning to come back to him. It was as if his family home was the key he'd needed to break through the fog that had clouded his mind for the last two days. He could feel it lifting out of his head, revealing the phantom shapes it had been hiding.

Sherlock noticed that something was wrong. 'Are you all right?' he asked.

Ed nodded and turned to look at him. 'I'm starting to remember,' he said. 'I remember... what happened to me.'

Sherlock smiled. 'That's excellent news,' he said. 'Well, it would appear we have a little time to kill. So why don't you tell me what happened? Tell me everything.'

NINETEEN

The Ransom

The boy had never been so scared in his entire life. His mouth was dry and his heart was hammering in his chest as he hurried away from the *Peveril of the Peak* and made his way towards the nearest tram stop with Lucky walking beside him. The dog was wagging his tail, delighted to be reunited with his owner and completely unaware of the awful situation in which the boy had suddenly found himself.

When he reached the stop a tram was just sliding in beside the platform, so he ran forward and managed to scramble aboard with only a few moments to spare before the doors slid shut. Luckily he'd already purchased a return ticket that morning so at least he didn't have to worry about an inspector getting on and arresting him for travelling without one, though right now that seemed the least of his worries.

On the slow, halting journey back to Chorlton, a thousand thoughts crashed and collided in his head like a major motorway accident. What if he couldn't get the safe open? What if the diamonds weren't in there? How did he know the grey-haired man would keep his promise and release Dad when he had the diamonds? He felt sick with worry and desperate to talk to somebody about his plight, but he didn't know anyone on the tram and wouldn't have known what to say to them even if he did.

When they finally got back to Chorlton he jumped out and ran all the way home, not daring to pause for breath. Once inside the house he removed Lucky's lead, filled a bowl with water for him and opened a tin of dog food, which he threw carelessly into another bowl. Lucky started eating as though he hadn't been fed in days and the boy hurried to his father's study and pulled back the carpet under his desk where he knew the safe was hidden. He lifted the hinged section of the floor, revealing the electronic keypad on the door of the metal box within. He pulled the scrap of paper from his pocket and keyed in the six digits, holding his breath as he did so. The safe emitted a harsh, metallic beep and for a moment he thought something was wrong. But then the latch clicked and he was able to pull open the heavy door. There were various things packed into the opening – padded brown envelopes, small gift boxes, reams of rolled paper encircled by elastic bands – but he soon identified what the grey-haired man had told him to fetch; a clear plastic bag containing a handful of tiny, glittering gems. He reached in, lifted the bag to the light of the window and saw that they were indeed pale pink in colour. This had to be them.

He closed the safe and stood up. He was about to stuff the diamonds into the pocket of his jeans then thought better of it. He imagined himself reaching in there for coins or something and inadvertently dropping the packet in the process. That would be a mistake he couldn't afford to make. Instead, he went to his bedroom and found the chunky metal whistle that he kept in his bedside locker. He had discovered years ago that it was possible to prise one side of the metal casing open to reveal a little hiding place within, where he could keep something small and precious. He took out the tiny metal locket that had belonged to his mum, the one with a tiny photograph of her inside, and placed it carefully in a drawer. When he pushed the plastic packet into the opening, the diamonds fit perfectly. He popped the side panel back into position with a soft click and hung the whistle around his neck. For extra safekeeping he tucked the whistle under his T-shirt.

He was ready to go. He threw a guilty glance at Lucky, knowing that he'd be expecting to go out for a run straight after eating, but that wasn't going to happen today. If Lucky had a little 'accident' on the rug later, it wouldn't be his fault. The boy paused to give the dog a reassuring pat and said, 'Wish me luck.' Then he let himself out of the house and ran all the way back to the tram stop. On the other side of the road a couple of friends shouted to him to stop and talk to them, but he ignored them and kept going.

He was gasping for breath by the time he got to the stop and saw to his annoyance that he'd just missed one tram and had twelve minutes to wait for the next. He paced anxiously up and down, glancing repeatedly at the illuminated display and seeing in his mind's eye the grey-haired man's furious expression as the minutes ticked steadily away. Finally the tram came into view, moving at an annoyingly sedate pace and as soon as the doors slid open he jumped aboard, reminding himself that this time he was only going as far as Piccadilly. Again, the questions crowded in on him. Where was he supposed to go when he got there? The man had said that somebody would be watching him until he arrived. But why had they chosen a busy place like the station? Was it so that the bad men could study him from a distance to ensure that he really had come alone?

He endured another slow, stop-start journey towards the city, unable to settle on anything as a thousand random thoughts careened through his mind. What if he took too long getting back? What if the tram was delayed? Had the bad men hurt Dad? How else would they have got the safe's combination off him?

The tram was already busy when he got on and as they moved steadily towards the city it got more and more crowded until the boy was jammed in amongst a press of people, all headed for the shops, the restaurants and the cinemas in the city centre. He felt sick, as though at any moment he might bring up his breakfast, but he knew he couldn't allow himself to do that; that was a complication he couldn't afford right now. He just had to get to the station and hand over the diamonds. His hand moved to the slight bulge of the whistle under his T-shirt, wanting to be sure it was still there, knowing that if he arrived without it something bad would happen to his father. The grey-haired man had told him so.

He knew, of course, that Dad was a diamond broker and that he often had to store valuable items at home, items that he'd purchased on behalf of one of his clients and from which he'd take a commission on the sale. It was the sort of work that Dad had always done, the same work *his* father had done before him and in all the years he'd been doing it, there'd never been a problem. The boy had occasionally asked Dad if it was safe having stuff like that at home, but Dad always told him there was absolutely nothing to worry about, he never told anybody what he did for a living, well, only his most trusted friends, and the other diamond brokers he worked with, so there was nothing to worry about on that score. But these men, these bad men had somehow found out about it. Maybe they'd overheard Dad talking to a client on the phone and afterwards had followed him home, worked out a way of getting to him. Maybe they'd been watching the house for ages, had seen the boy walking Lucky and realised that here was a really sneaky way to get to those diamonds.

Lucky had vanished a week earlier. One morning, the boy let him out onto the stretch of land in front of the house for his usual wee. He'd let him out of the door and then turned back a moment to scoop up the last bit of cereal in his breakfast bowl and when he'd come out, with the lead in his hand, there was no sign of Lucky, he'd just vanished as though he'd been spirited away. And that must have been the men, the boy told himself, waiting in the trees, watching the house and looking for an opportunity to grab Lucky and run off with him...

The tram jolted to a halt at some lights and the boy came back to the present. They were on the outskirts of Manchester now, the pavements teeming with shoppers, people going happily about their lives, not suspecting for a moment that in their midst was a boy going through the worst experience of his life. He wanted to scream and shout, but he couldn't do that. He had to keep things together for Dad's sake...

Finally, the tram trundled into the short stretch of tunnel that led to Piccadilly Station and emerged alongside the crowded platform. The doors slid open and the people on board moved as one, all seemingly in a hurry to alight as quickly as possible. The boy found himself wedged in the midst of a sea of humanity, one hand held protectively over the whistle under his T-shirt. Then he was on the platform and heading for the escalator. He reached the foot of it, found a spot on the right hand side and tried to angle his head to the left to see past the people standing in front of him. Just then there was a commotion from behind him as a man carrying a huge backpack shouted something about a train leaving in two minutes. The man stepped to his left and charged past the boy, beckoning to somebody just behind him and telling him to get a move on.

The boy turned to look just as a second man came charging up the escalator, he too, burdened by a huge backpack. As the man went past, his pack lurched to one side and the boy just had time to register the bulk of it swinging towards his face before something hard connected with the side of his head, with a powerful whack, almost knocking him clean off his feet. He swung to his right, fell against the rail, dazed and shocked, but managed to correct himself and got upright again, just in time to see the big man blundering on up the escalator, his unruly pack buffeting other people as he went by. Somebody shouted to him to be more careful.

And then the boy felt the strangest sensation. There was a dull pain in the side of his head and it was as though somebody had pulled a tab on the side of his face, allowing a thick fog to spurt into it, a fog that spread outwards in a grey blanket to completely obscure everything that was in his mind. He blinked, stared straight ahead, telling himself that he had to keep control of himself because he was here for something really important, he was here to... to... he was here to...

He arrived at the top of the escalator and almost fell as moving metal melted into stone tiles, but there were people behind him, pushing him and complaining at his indecision, so he kept moving forward, shaking his head to try and dispel the fog that had swamped him. But the more he did that, the thicker the fog became and now, now he really didn't know why he was here and could only tell himself that he must have come to catch a train because this was obviously a station, right? And that's what you did at stations.

He tried to stop walking for a moment, but somebody behind him jostled him and told him to watch what he was doing so he stumbled onwards and turned a corner. Another escalator lay ahead of him, leading up to the main station concourse, somewhere he thought he recognised and he went with the crowd, realising with a dull twinge of surprise that he didn't know anything.

I don't know my own name. The thought flashed across his mind and he almost giggled at the madness of it. How could he not know that? How? He struggled to locate it in the fog.

My name is… my name…

As he came to the top of the escalator he noticed a man leaning on a rail nearby, watching the people as they rode up. The man was skinny with thick wiry hair, bulging eyes and oddly, no brows. This struck the boy as important. It seemed to him that it ought to mean something to him, but it didn't really, it just looked strange. And then he noticed that the man was staring at him with those big, bulging eyes and he nodded to the boy as if in greeting. He straightened up and walked closer to the escalator, as though intending to intercept him.

The boy didn't check his pace. He stepped off the escalator and started walking straight ahead, aiming himself for the big illuminated display board that he could see up ahead of him in the centre of the station concourse. The man frowned. 'Hey,' he said. 'You got something for me?'

The boy shook his head, kept walking, following a piece of advice in his head, even though he didn't know who'd given him the advice in the first place.

If a stranger tries to talk to you, just walk away and look for a policeman.

The boy scanned the crowds helplessly but there was no policeman in sight. He glanced back and saw that the goggle-eyed man was gesturing up towards the balcony over to his left and when the boy looked, he saw another man standing up there, frowning down at the crowds below – a grey-haired man in a suede coat with a sheepskin collar. It seemed to the boy that this man was familiar too, but he couldn't say from where and now, he saw that the man was leaving his position up on the balcony and walking quickly towards a flight of steps that led down to platform level.

'Hey!' The goggle-eyed man spoke again, sounding angry now. 'Where do you think you're going?'

The boy looked around, the pain in his head making him feel as though his skull was about to split. To his right he saw the glass doors leading to the platforms and instinctively he headed towards them, sensing that through there he might find some avenue of escape. It seemed to him that if he went through this entrance and out to the far side of the station there would be another exit, one which might get him out of here, away from the two men who were following him. He didn't know exactly how he knew this, only that he was sure he'd used it before. The goggle-eyed man saw his intention and quickened his pace. 'You little idiot, come back 'ere,' he barked. The boy turned his head, saw Goggle-Eyes breaking into a run, and a short distance behind him Grey-Hair was pushing his way through the crowd, a furious look on his face. The boy panicked and ran towards the nearest glass doorway. It slid open automatically and he went through, noticing that there were trains standing at nearly every platform ahead of him, but he ignored them and headed away to his right where a couple of men in high visibility jackets stood in front of a narrow entrance. The boy was past them before they even knew what was happening and he ignored their shouts, but turned his head briefly when he heard other voices, only to see that the men had spun around to intercept Goggle-Eyes and Grey Hair, demanding to see their tickets. The two men were waving their arms, pointing to the boy. They were trying to struggle free and now more men in yellow jackets came running to help hold them.

The boy didn't stop to try and explain. He kept

running until he came to a travelator which led him to a smaller concourse, where neon signs told him about trains leaving from two more platforms. He noticed a young couple running frantically towards an exit, pulling heavy suitcases behind them, as though they were late for something and sheep-like he followed them, turned a corner and overtook them on a flight of stairs that led down to yet another level. A train was standing at the platform and as he reached ground level he heard the shrill beeping sound of electronic doors as they began to slide shut. Without thinking, he aimed himself for the narrowly closing gap and jumped aboard. The door clunked shut just behind him and he turned, saw the young couple struggling onto the platform a few moments too late, their expressions furious.

Now the train moved slowly away and the boy waited by the door, peering anxiously through the glass to see if Goggle-Eyes and Grey-Hair would reappear but they didn't. So the boy went into the nearest carriage and found an empty seat at a table, opposite an elderly couple. The woman smiled at him in a friendly way but he slumped into his seat and turned his head to look out of the window. His skull felt as though it was splitting in two and all of a sudden, he was tired, really tired.

At Oxford Road, a middle-aged businessman got on and took the seat beside him, but he was so exhausted by now that he barely registered the man's presence.

His eyes felt heavy and they came down like two heavy shutters, cutting off the light. The fog deepened and settled in his head and he slept as the train sped across the countryside.

TWENTY

Reinforcements

'You know the rest,' murmured Ed.

Sherlock nodded. 'What made you suddenly remember?' he asked.

'I think it was seeing my house up close.' Ed nodded at the building across the road. 'It all came back to me in a rush.' He reached up and rubbed the still tender area on the side of his head. 'I remember nearly everything now. My dad's name is Michael. And my mother, well, she was called Theresa. But she died in a car accident when I was only little.'

Sherlock frowned. 'I'm sorry to hear that,' he said.

'It's ok. It happened a long time ago.' Ed sighed. 'I hardly ever think of her now. There's just one thing I still don't know.'

'What's that?' asked Sherlock.

'My name. I don't know my real name. I keep trying to remember it, but it won't come to me.'

'I'm pretty sure we'll have that before very much longer,' Sherlock promised him, waving the binoculars. 'The figure sitting on the sofa is almost certainly your father.'

'But... why do you think he's praying like that?'

'I don't believe he is. I imagine his hands are tied together in front of him.'

'Oh. Right.' Ed felt rather stupid. It hadn't occurred to him that this might be the case. 'So... *that's* why Lucky is sitting beside him,' he said. 'Trying to look after him. I guess it makes sense.'

Just then, a portal appeared in the air in front of them, making its usual high-pitched whining sound, the air rippling and swaying around it. 'Ah,' said Sherlock turning towards it. 'This must be the first of our reinforcements. Let's hope James has chosen wisely.'

Ed stared at the opening in amazement as a familiar shape materialised in the midst of it, the bronze statue of a man in uniform sitting astride a huge black horse. Sultan came through the portal in an elegant leap and thudded onto the soft ground. He stood there, tossing his head and stamping his feet, as though ready to run off at any moment. 'Whoah, boy, settle down!' The Colonel looked this way and that, a startled expression on his moustachioed face. Then he saw the two figures standing a short distance away.

'Mr Holmes!' he snapped. 'What is the meaning of this outrage? What on earth is going on?'

Sherlock stepped forward. 'I apologise, Colonel Alexander. I hope you know I wouldn't have had you brought here if it wasn't absolutely essential.' He indicated Ed. 'I shan't introduce you as I know you two have already met.'

'But what… what on earth is happening? A moment ago I was riding Sultan along the Royal Mile and now…'

'Yes, so I see. I wasn't really expecting you to bring your horse with you, but I'm sure he will be useful. It's rather hard to explain how I got you here and I'm afraid I…' The portal started whining again, suggesting that somebody else was about to come through. 'If you'd just ride clear of the portal a moment, Colonel Alexander, I think somebody else is about to arrive.'

'Most extraordinary,' muttered the Colonel, but he wheeled Sultan aside and rode him to a safe distance as a second figure began to materialise in the opening.

'Oh no,' Ed heard Sherlock mutter and an instant later he understood what the problem was, because now the tall, stone statue of a man in armour was striding through the portal. He stood, looking around open-mouthed in astonishment. Then, with a brief ripping sound, the portal snapped shut behind him. He whipped around as though sensing an attack from the rear, but when he saw nothing he twisted back again, his expression fierce. William Wallace stared across the clearing at Sherlock. 'You!' he snarled. 'I might have known you'd have something to do with this.' He took a threatening step forward, his sword raised.

'Great choice, James,' muttered Sherlock, but he moved forward, his arms raised in surrender. 'Will, this is not the time or the place,' he protested. 'Please, lower your weapon. I've had you and Colonel Alexander sent here to help me out with a very important mission.'

William hesitated and looked around in astonishment. 'Help *you*?' he growled. 'Now why would I do a thing like that? And... sent where?' he bellowed. 'Where, in the name of Lucifer, am I?'

'In er... in Manchester,' said Sherlock.

'Manchester, *England*?' cried William in disbelief.

'I'm afraid so. Look, I know it's not ideal but...'

'How can we possibly be in England?' interrupted the Colonel, guiding Sultan closer. 'Only two moments ago I was in Edinburgh. I was riding along, minding my own business...'

'Me too,' said William. 'Well, I wasn't riding, I was walking. And then all of a sudden I went all muckle-headed.' He glared at Sherlock. 'It's witchcraft!' he roared. 'He's set an enchantment on us.'

'No, William, it's science. I appreciate that for you it amounts to pretty much the same thing but trust me, I...'

'Why would I trust you, ye heathen *Sassenach*?'

'Mr Wallace, please!' cried the Colonel. 'Let's have a bit of decorum, shall we? Let's not forget we are gentlemen.' He studied Ed for a moment. 'Does this have something to do with the boy?' he asked.

'Yes, it does.' Sherlock opened his arms in an attempt to appeal to the two newcomers. He pointed across the road. 'In that cottage over the way, bad men are holding this boy's father hostage…'

'And my dog,' added Ed.

'Yes, and his… er, dog. There are five men in there, all armed with guns…'

'What kind of men?' asked William.

'They are… bad men,' said Sherlock.

'*Englishmen*?' growled William.

'Er… yes. They *are* Englishmen, actually. *Bad* Englishmen.'

'Is there any other kind?' murmured William.

'Well, yes there is, but that's a very complicated discussion, best kept for another time. This boy here, he's been treated most cruelly by these villains. With your help, I wish to bring them to justice.'

'So… you're telling me that you've managed to work out who the boy is,' said the Colonel, looking impressed. 'And you've brought him back to his home, just as the king asked you to.'

'That's right,' agreed Sherlock.

'Using witchcraft,' said William.

'No, I promise you it's not witchcraft, but of course,

it must seem pretty fantastic to you. Suffice to say that James Clerk Maxwell has invented a method of getting people from one place to another…'

'Clerk Maxwell?' muttered William. 'I've heard all about him. He's a dark magician!' He spat on the ground.

'He's not,' interrupted Ed. 'I've met him. He's just… very clever. And the machine he made really does work.'

There was a short silence while the two men considered this information.

'So… what do you want us to do exactly?' asked the Colonel.

Sherlock pointed once again to the house. 'I want you to attack that house…'

'Yes! Why didn't you say so earlier?' William pumped a gloved fist into the air. He looked as though he was about to race straight across the road and go to work, but Sherlock managed to restrain him.

'Wait! Wait just a minute! I need to explain the situation to you both. It's not as straightforward as you might think.'

William scowled but turned back to listen.

'I want you to overpower the five men in that house. But at the same time, you must protect the boy's father. He's the one who is tied up in there. Seriously, no harm must come to him.'

'Or my dog,' added Ed.

'Yes, please watch out for his dog too,' added Sherlock. 'He's very special.'

'Is the boy's father an Englishmen?' asked William slyly.

'Er… no, he's Scottish, born and bred,' lied Sherlock and ignored the incredulous look that Ed gave him 'Though his accent may *sound* a little bit English due to the fact that he's lived here for so many years.'

'Hmm.' William looked far from impressed. 'We all make bad choices in life, I suppose. And the bad men? Are we allowed to…' He made a hacking motion with his sword.

'Oh no,' said Sherlock hastily. 'I don't mind if you thump them a bit but I want them alive, preferably tied up so they can't do any harm.'

'And where are you going to be, Mr Holmes, while all this is going on?' enquired the Colonel.

'I'll be right behind you,' Sherlock told him. 'Ordinarily, of course, I'd have taken them on myself…'

'Oh, I'm *sure* you would,' sneered William.

'Yes, really, but I have to be sure that neither the boy or his father…'

'Or his dog!'

'Yes, thank you, Ed. I have to be sure that none of them are injured. And I can't guarantee to do that when there are five villains to take care of. They may have orders to harm the boy's father if anything goes wrong. Or indeed, the boy himself. As a father yourself, Mr

Wallace, I know you'll appreciate how awful that would be.'

William looked suddenly rather misty-eyed. 'It's a terrible thing, the loss of your loved ones,' he said. 'The worst thing that can happen to a man. It can unhinge you. It can make you demented. It's the only bit of the film they got right,' he added mysteriously. Then he coughed, as though embarrassed to have shown a more human side of his nature. 'I appreciate your concern,' he said grudgingly. 'Don't worry, I'll ensure all innocent parties remain unharmed. But if those Englishmen push me too hard then, by heaven's flames, I shall…'

'Just be circumspect,' Sherlock advised him.

'I don't know what that means,' said William, looking baffled.

'I didn't either,' Ed reassured him. 'I think it just means "careful".'

'Er… yes, quite. Be very careful.' Sherlock clapped his huge hands together. 'Now, William, if you would be good enough to cover the back of the house. And Colonel Alexander, if you would take the front?'

'What about me?' asked Ed.

'You?' Sherlock looked down at him. 'You'll stay here where you'll be safe.'

'No way! I'm not letting you go in there without me.'

'I really don't think…'

'Let the lad go in!' said William. 'It's *his* father in there!'

'And my dog.'

Sherlock sighed. 'Oh, all right, but I want you to stay close behind me. The last thing we need is for you to be injured.'

'We're going to be seen, you know,' the Colonel reminded him. He indicated the road along which the occasional car was passing. 'By softies,' he added, in case anyone was in any doubt.

'I appreciate that,' said Sherlock. 'It's not ideal but I'm afraid that's something we're just going to have to accept. Once we're inside and the villains are safely overpowered, I'll arrange for a portal to appear inside the house and the two of you will be sent straight back to where you came from.'

'By witchcraft?' cried William.

'No, by science! I wish you'd stop using that word. It's most inaccurate. Now, if you'll excuse me for a moment, I've a few preparations to make.' He turned away, pulling out his mobile phone as he did so. The Colonel took the opportunity to edge Sultan a little closer to Ed.

'So, lad, how have you been since I last saw you?' he asked.

'Good, thanks,' murmured Ed.

'Clearly, Mr Holmes isn't the idiot he's been painted.'

'Oh, he's not,' agreed Ed. 'He's... brilliant, really. He worked out everything, just like the real Sherlock Holmes.'

'There *was* no real Sherlock Holmes,' the Colonel

reminded him. 'Which is, I suppose, one reason why so many of us statues don't trust him. But I take your point. And it appears that he's done a thorough job. I'll certainly give a good report back to Charlie.'

Ed made a face. 'Don't talk to me about *him*! He sent a couple of Gormleys after me. They tried to kill me.'

'He did what?' The Colonel looked shocked. 'But that's outrageous! He pardoned you. Everybody in Parliament Square heard him do it.'

'Well, I'm not making it up, honest. They fired arrows at me. If it hadn't been for Sherlock, I'd probably be dead now.'

The Colonel tutted loudly. 'But that's terrible! A king should never go back on his word. Wait till I tell David about this,' he added. 'I've no doubt he'll have something to say about the situation.' He looked up as Sherlock came back, slipping the phone into his pocket as he did so. 'The boy gives a good account of you, Mr Holmes,' said the Colonel. 'It would appear you have indeed proved yourself to be more than just talk.'

'Thank you,' said Sherlock, bowing his head. 'One does one's best.'

'Don't give him any more compliments,' warned William. 'The man already has far too high an opinion of his own abilities.'

'It's all arranged,' said Sherlock, ignoring the jibe. 'I've just spoken to James Clerk Maxwell and…'

'How have you done that?' cried William. 'He's in Edinburgh.'

'I know, but I have a device that enables me to speak over long distances. And don't say that's witchcraft because I know you must have observed humans using them all the time.' He looked from William to the Colonel and back again. 'Now… gentlemen, if you would prepare yourselves?'

'Always ready for battle,' said the Colonel.

'And always ready to crack some *Sassenach* skulls,' added William.

'Just… take it gently,' suggested Sherlock and then rolled his eyes, clearly appreciating how unlikely an occurrence *that* was. 'William, if you'd like to head around the back first? Try to stay out of sight of the people inside. When you hear the sound of Colonel Alexander going in at the front door, you will do likewise at the back.'

'Oh, don't you worry about me,' said William. 'I was born for things like this.' He turned to gaze malevolently towards the cottage.

'On my count,' said Sherlock. 'One… two…' But William was already gone, racing out of the trees and across the road, passing a couple of startled pedestrians as he did so. He vaulted nimbly over the garden gate, then stooped below the level of the windows and went around the back, out of sight. The pedestrians, an elderly couple, moved slowly onwards, looking repeatedly back towards the cottage as though they couldn't quite believe the evidence of their own eyes.

'We'll give him a few moments to take up his position,' suggested Sherlock.

The Colonel nodded. He reached out a gloved hand and stroked Sultan's neck. 'Reminds me of the old days,' he said, softly. 'It's been a while since I was involved in a glorious charge. Shame there's just the one of me. It would have been nice to ride alongside some of my old comrades.'

'I've no doubt you'll be more than enough,' Sherlock assured him. 'Ready?'

The Colonel nodded.

'Go!' The Colonel spurred his mount and Sultan took off through the trees, heading straight towards the cottage. As he crossed the pavement onto the road, he narrowly missed colliding with a car, which blared its horn, but kept on going. Sherlock winced. 'That was too close for comfort,' he said. He glanced down at Ed. 'Stay right behind me,' he warned the boy. And he too strode towards the cottage with Ed hanging on to the back of his coat. As they crossed the road, Ed peeped out under Sherlock's right arm and saw that Sultan had just taken a mighty leap and cleared the garden fence. He came down hard on the path, the impact of his bronze hooves cracking the concrete, but he didn't slow his pace and thundered headlong towards the cottage door. There was an ear-splitting crash and it smashed open on impact, the lock shattered. The Colonel ducked his head and he and Sultan raced inside.

Almost instantly there was another crash from the back of the house, closely followed by shouts of alarm and the sound of guns firing. By then Sherlock was kicking open the gate and running up the path. Ed stayed with him, matching him step for step. They went through the open doorway and found themselves in a scene of complete chaos. Sultan looked huge in the tiny lounge and the Colonel was leaning over in his saddle, mostly to avoid banging his head on the low ceiling. As Ed watched, the Colonel knocked a burly-looking man flat on his back with one almighty punch. Over at the equally shattered back door, William Wallace was in the act of picking a muscle-bound fellow up by the scruff of his neck. William gave a great bellow and flung the man clear across the room. He crashed into a wall behind Ed and came down in a tangle of arms and legs, taking a rather nice painting with him.

There were shouts of alarm from upstairs and William made a beeline in that direction, racing up the staircase with his sword held in front of him. There was a brief commotion up there, the sounds of things being smashed and, moments later, a third man came tumbling head over heels down the stairs before crashing headlong into the banister rail at the bottom. He groaned, tried to stagger to his feet, but sank down again and lay still.

'Everybody freeze!'

Ed snapped his head around and saw his father, still sitting on the sofa, his hands tied in front of him. A fourth man, a big, bearded fellow in a red t-shirt was sitting beside him, a brawny arm around his neck and a gun held to his head.

For a moment everything was silent. The bearded

man was looking around in evident terror, clearly unsure of what was happening here but determined to save his own skin by any means possible. The gun in his hand was shaking and looked as though it could go off at any moment. Dad's expression was also one of astonishment. He was staring around the room and seemed barely aware of the gun jammed against the side of his head.

'The jig's up,' said Sherlock, speaking with surprising calmness to the bearded man. 'Put the gun down and come quietly.'

The man shook his head. 'Stay back,' he said. 'Stay back or I'll shoot.'

'That would be a mistake,' said Sherlock. 'You're outnumbered, you can't hope to…'

'Back away from the door! I mean it. Me and him are walking out of here and if anybody tries to stop us, they…'

He broke off in surprise as suddenly, shockingly, Lucky leapt over the arm of the sofa and fastened his jaws around the man's gun arm, wrenching him hard to one side. The weapon went off with a loud bang and a brief flash of light but the bullet thudded harmlessly into the floor by Dad's feet. Then Lucky had the bearded man down on the floor and was tearing at his arm as though it was a juicy bone. He bellowed in pain and fright.

Sherlock stepped forward and brought his fist down hard on the gunman's head, knocking him senseless.

He slumped, unconscious, and Lucky backed away from him, growling at the back of his throat as though daring him to get up again. Sherlock crouched and removed the gun from the man's hand. There was one last shout from upstairs, a couple more gunshots, then a long deep silence. Everybody's gaze snapped to the top of the stairs. After a few moments William appeared, a no-nonsense expression on his face.

'Piece of cake,' he said. 'They barely put up a struggle.' He looked hopefully around. 'Anybody else need thumping?' he asked hopefully.

Ed finally had time to turn his attention to the man on the sofa. He was looking around the room in sheer open-mouthed disbelief as though he'd suddenly found himself rescued from one nightmare and plunged straight into another one. Ed stepped out from behind Sherlock and his father's gaze finally found his.

'Sam!' he cried.

The boy who was once called Ed, looked up at Sherlock and grinned. 'Sam,' he said. 'Now I've heard it, I know it's right.' He ran to the sofa and threw his arms around his dad. A moment later, Lucky was there too, licking Sam's face and yelping with delight.

William came slowly down the stairs and leaned on the broken banister rail, gazing proudly around at the cottage's wrecked interior. 'Now that's what I call a result,' he said.

TWENTY ONE

Aftermath

There wasn't an awful lot of time to sort things out. Sherlock got straight back on the phone and asked James to provide a portal. William Wallace chose to go back first, but not before he'd given Sherlock a meaningful look. 'You owe me now,' he said. 'Don't think I'm going to forget that.'

'I'm sure you won't,' said Sherlock.

'The next time we meet in Edinburgh, I'll expect you to come out and face me man-to-man.'

'You can depend on it,' Sherlock told him. He reached out and shook William's hand. Then he indicated the portal, which was shimmering and rippling in mid-air in the centre of the lounge. Meanwhile, Sam and his dad sat on the sofa, watching in silence. Dad's expression was still one of total disbelief.

'I just… step through it?' muttered William.

'That's right,' Sherlock assured him. 'It won't hurt a bit.'

'Witchcraft,' said William and he spat on the carpet to make his point. But he turned towards the portal and started singing as he walked towards it.

> *'I have brought ye to the ring*
> *Now dance if ye can!*
> *I have brought ye to the revel*
> *Now see if ye can…'*

He passed through the portal and was gone in a flash of light. Sherlock turned his head. 'Colonel Alexander?' he murmured. 'You're next.'

The Colonel edged Sultan closer to the portal. He paused for a moment and looked down at Sherlock. 'Well, Mr Holmes, it's been a brief but pleasant interval. I shall report back about Charlie's devious ways. I'm sure it won't sit well with a lot of statues.' He glanced over at Sam. 'As for you, young man, it's been a pleasure to make your acquaintance. I'm glad you got yourself sorted out.'

'Thanks, Colonel,' said Sam. 'And say hello to David for me.' He turned to look at his dad. 'That's David Livingstone,' he added. 'He saved me from having my head chopped off.'

'Did he?' said Dad. 'That's nice.'

'Giddy up, lad!' The Colonel urged Sultan towards

the portal and they leapt through the opening. For a moment he was frozen in the entrance, looking every inch the heroic cavalry officer, then he too was gone in another flare of brilliant white light. Sherlock stood for a moment and looked quickly around the room, appraising the situation. The place looked like it had been hit by a bomb and the five unconscious villains were stretched out where they'd fallen, each one of them tied with a length of washing line that William had foraged from the back garden. Sherlock looked apologetically at Sam's dad. 'I'm sorry about the mess,' he said. 'I had hoped it wouldn't be quite as bad as this. But the main thing is, you're all unharmed and I've no doubt your possessions must be insured.'

Dad was finally trying to find some words. 'I don't … what… I mean, what the… who the… what *is* this?' he cried at last. 'What's going on?'

Sherlock smiled. 'I'm sure Sam will explain it all after I'm gone,' he said. 'Though I'll tell you now, it isn't going to make an awful lot of sense. You know what they say. Life is infinitely stranger than anything which the mind of man could invent.' He glanced towards the shattered doorway. They'd managed to close it after a fashion, but through the front window of the house they could all see a small group of curious people gathered at the end of the garden path, alerted by the sounds of gunfire from within the cottage. 'Somebody must surely have called the police by now,' added Sherlock, 'so I daren't stick around for very much longer.' He gestured towards the portal. 'And I do have a few things to sort out at home.'

Sam got up off the sofa. 'You're going back to Edinburgh?' he asked. He realised in that moment that he was about to lose somebody who had become a very good friend. 'Do you really have to go straight away?'

'I'm afraid so,' said Sherlock. 'If the police find me here, it'll be beyond all rational explanation.'

'And how will we explain all *this*?' asked Sam, gesturing around the devastated lounge.

Sherlock smiled and looked at Sam's dad. 'Here's the story,' he said. 'It's not the very best, but we don't have time to invent a decent one. You, sir... I'm sorry, I still don't know your full name, Mr...?'

'Watson. Michael Watson.'

Sherlock turned to look at Sam in amazement. 'Your name is Watson?' he cried. 'Sam Watson?'

Sam looked apologetic. 'Er... yeah. Of course, I didn't know that before. It only came back to me a few minutes ago. Is it... is it a problem?'

'Not at all. I think it's a wonderful coincidence. It's just a wonder you're not called *John* Watson.'

'John is my middle name,' said Sam, sheepishly, and Sherlock laughed in sheer disbelief.

'When you grow up, perhaps you should enter the medical profession,' he said. 'Then you can genuinely call yourself Dr Watson!' He had to make a real effort to get back to his original subject. He turned back to look at Sam's dad. 'You, sir, are a martial arts expert.'

'I am?' murmured Dad. He sounded dazed, like he'd just woken from a deep sleep.

'You are indeed. You have practised it since you were a small boy. Whilst being held prisoner here, you somehow managed to get free from your bonds and you overpowered all five of these villains by sheer brute force.'

'Who'll believe that?' murmured Dad.

'Well, you *could* try telling the police what actually happened,' said Sherlock. 'Though seriously, I wouldn't recommend it. The danger is people will think you're unhinged.'

'I'm beginning to wonder that myself,' said Dad.

'Oh, don't worry. Once you've managed to get a little distance from this, it will start to make some kind of sense. Probably.' Sherlock turned towards the portal and Sam stepped closer, and hung onto his arm.

'You can't just leave,' he said. 'Not yet.'

'I'm rather afraid I have to,' said Sherlock. 'I'm sorry. It would have been lovely to stay a little longer and see the sights here in your wonderful city, but... well, I'm afraid my work here is done.' He reached out a huge gloved hand and shook Sam's tiny human one in his. 'Look,' he said, 'If you're ever up in Edinburgh, you know where to find me.'

The sound of a siren snatched his gaze to the window. A police car was pulling up by the gate and the small crowd was shouting and pointing towards the house. 'Oh, I nearly forgot,' said Sherlock. He reached into his waistcoat pocket and pulled out the metal whistle. He handed it to Sam. 'There you are,' he said. 'I have a feeling that this is important to you. I shouldn't be at all surprised if it normally holds something very precious.'

'Thanks,' murmured Sam. 'I thought that got left at the Hippodrome.' He took the whistle and hung it back around his neck.

'I picked it up before we left,' Sherlock told him. 'Attention to detail is so important in my line of work.'

'I wish you *could* stay,' Sam added.

'Me too,' said Sherlock. 'And I really didn't expect to be saying that. I'm usually such a solitary kind of fellow.' He smiled. 'Well, good luck, Sam Watson. And remember, both of you. Just stick to the story, no matter how many questions they fire at you. Nothing clears up a case so much as stating it to another person. Now… farewell!'

With that he stepped into the portal. There was a last brief flash of intense light followed by a loud zipping sound. And he was gone, leaving no sign that he had ever been there.

Sam stood in the centre of the room looking at the place where the portal had been. He was astonished to find that his eyes felt itchy and when he lifted a hand to his face he was aware of a single tear coursing its way down his cheek.

'What just happened?' asked Dad.

'It's a long story,' Sam warned him, wiping the tear

away with the sleeve of his jacket. 'But I *will* tell you all about it, the first chance I get. Promise.'

He turned at the sound of a furious rapping on the broken door.

'I'll get that,' he said.

TWENTY TWO

Epilogue

It was exactly one year later. Sam and his father strolled slowly along Leith Walk. The madness of the Edinburgh Festival had finally subsided as the hours stretched themselves into darkness. Sam kept glancing at his watch. It was eight minutes to midnight and his excitement was steadily mounting. They reached the little square at Picardy Place and there was Sherlock, standing up on his plinth, his pipe gripped in one hand, his eyes fixed straight ahead.

'I can't believe I let you talk me into this,' said Dad.

Sam smiled. He indicated a wooden bench just a short distance from the statue and he and his dad took a seat. They sat there, staring up at the bronze detective. Sam had worked on Dad steadily throughout the year, reminding him, nagging him, telling him that he had to let him do this, it was the only thing he wanted, it would do instead of a birthday or a Christmas present. On August the second, come hell or high water, he had to be in Edinburgh.

'I don't know what you think is going to happen,' insisted Dad.

'Maybe nothing,' said Sam. 'Maybe we'll just blink and then we'll go back to the hotel.'

Over the year, Dad had somehow managed to convince himself that he'd been suffering from hallucinations in that moment when Sam had arrived with reinforcements; that what had happened in the cottage must have all been in his head. Because it was insane, when you thought about it. Statues didn't move. Statues didn't talk. And they certainly didn't step through portals and vanish into thin air. Sam had allowed him to think whatever he wanted, but he'd still quietly insisted that he wouldn't take no for an answer. This year's holiday would have to be a trip to the Edinburgh Festival.

Sam glanced again at his watch. One minute to midnight. He didn't know what he'd do if he just blinked and suddenly it was 12.01. He supposed he'd have to live with it, but he also knew that the disappointment would be absolutely crushing. He'd been anticipating this moment all year long. There was unfinished business here and he didn't want to leave it that way.

The last few seconds ticked by and he held his breath.

'What happens if…?' Dad's question was interrupted by the tolling of an iron bell, somewhere off in the distance. Sam waited for Dad to continue but he didn't and when Sam looked at him, his saw that his father's eyes were closed and his chest was rising and falling rhythmically.

'Dad?' Sam lifted a hand to shake his father's shoulder but he didn't wake. 'Dad?' He was sleeping very soundly.

Just then there was a clattering sound from the direction of the road and Sam lifted his head to look. Two tall spindly shapes were racing madly along the road, their metal hooves striking sparks in the gloom. Sam got up from the bench for a better look as they clattered on by, their cable tails lashing.

'Dreaming Spires,' he murmured.

'The zoo,' said a familiar voice in the air above him and he turned in surprise to look up at Sherlock. The bronze detective was smiling down at him. 'They go to the zoo. I worked it out. It came to me quite suddenly in February. It was elementary. After all, where else would creatures go when they think they're giraffes? They can't make it all the way to Africa, can they?'

Sam grinned delightedly. 'It worked,' he said. 'I'm here.'

'Of course you are! Mind you, we still don't really know *why*.' Sherlock slipped the pipe into his pocket and clambered carefully down off his plinth. He had a bit of a stretch and then came closer. 'You're no longer suffering from amnesia so we can eliminate the Colonel's theory. It must have been something that happened to your brain when you got that bump on the noggin. Something permanent, perhaps.' He towered over Sam, smiling down at him. 'So, how's Ed?' he asked.

'He's gone. I'm Sam Watson now.'

'I appreciate that, but to some of us you'll always be Ed Fest.' Sherlock smiled, glanced over to the bench where Dad was still fast asleep. 'So you managed to talk him into coming here. How has he been?'

'Oh, he's been okay. He's back at work and everything. But he doesn't really believe it all happened.'

Sherlock chuckled. 'I can't say I blame him. And how did everything go after I er... left?'

Sam shrugged. 'It was complicated. The police didn't really believe our story, but we stuck to it, like you told us to, even when some of the neighbours said they'd seen...' He couldn't help chuckling. '... statues going into the house.'

'As if such a thing could happen!'

'But it's like I told them... once you eliminate the impossible, whatever remains, however improbable, must be the truth.'

Sherlock smiled. 'You're learning, my dear Watson... and I suspect you've been reading some of Sir Arthur's stories.'

Sam grinned. 'Yeah, I've read a few of them now. They're really good.'

'And what happened to Myles and his unsavoury crew?'

'They went to jail. Myles was really called Tobias, by the way, and he worked for the same firm as my dad, just like you figured. Turned out he had all these gambling debts and he was trying to buy his way out of trouble.'

Sherlock nodded. 'I thought it would be something like that,' he said. 'It all sounds depressingly typical.' He looked thoughtful. 'So, what's the plan?' he asked. 'You've managed to be here for another Calling, so…'

'I'd like to visit everyone,' said Sam eagerly. 'All my friends here, I mean. The Colonel, David Livingstone… even Mad Willy.'

'Well, I'm perfectly happy to act as your guide,' said Sherlock. 'And I know James has been dying to ask you a few questions.'

'Brilliant,' said Sam. 'I'm up for that.' He glanced at his dad's still form, sitting on the wooden bench. 'Will he be okay?' he asked.

'Of course he will. We'll have you back here at midnight, I'll pop back on my plinth, and he'll wake as soon as the bells chime. He'll think he's simply blinked.' Sherlock thought for a moment. 'It's probably best if you pretend that's all that happened to you too. Act disappointed. You can do that, can't you?'

Sam nodded. 'Sure. And…'

'Yes?'

'Well, I was thinking… this time around, I wouldn't

mind calling at the Agon. I'd like to see what goes on there.'

Sherlock sighed. 'Well, as it happens, I'm actually planning to attend the ceremony this year.'

Sam was surprised to hear this. 'You are? But I thought you hated it.'

'I do, rather, but this year's a bit different. I'm being given some kind of... medal. For valour.'

'Wow. How did you get that?'

'By helping you, of course! Colonel Alexander put in a good word for me. Oh, you know these military types, they love handing out medals! Of course it was too late to organise anything for last year. But I was told by several statues what they had planned for me this time, just before I climbed back on my plinth. Apparently Sir Walter told everyone last year that he was planning to compose a heroic ballad about my adventures in Manchester.' Sherlock made a face. 'One has to be polite, but it sounds like an awful prospect.'

'And what will Charlie have to say about it?'

'Ah! Charlie can't say very much at all,' said Sherlock. 'You see, when I got back last time, the Colonel was already telling people about the king's dastardly attempts to have you silenced. It caused some bad feeling. Statues are supposed to stand by their word of honour, especially when they're royalty. Apparently, at last year's Agon there was a big scene when David Livingstone stood up and denounced the king in front of everyone! After that, there was a public vote and it was decided that Charles and Victoria should rule together in future, so that neither could embark on any action without the agreement of the other.'

'Wow. That's big,' said Sam.

'It is indeed.' Sherlock smiled with evident pleasure. 'It's already been implemented. Of course, you will still need to keep an eye out for Charlie. He'll doubtless blame you for his downfall and he's not the sort to forget a slight easily. At the same time, he can't do anything too obvious or he'll bring even more disapproval down on his head. He'd need to be...'

'Circumspect?' suggested Sam and they both laughed.

'Suffice to say, if Charlie isn't very careful, Victoria could well be ruling the city alone by next year.'

'Oh, we should visit her too,' suggested Sam. 'She was cool.'

'Why not? She's only a little way up the road. Why don't we begin with her?' Sherlock started walking and Sam fell into step alongside him. 'She'll doubtless be getting ready for her annual visit from Prince Albert, but I'm sure she'll spare us a few moments.'

'This time, I'll have the whole twenty-four hours,' said Sam, eagerly.

Sherlock nodded. 'You know, we could think about making this a yearly event,' he said. 'Provided of course, you don't lose the gift of staying awake when the bell chimes.'

'Do you suppose it might wear off one day?' asked

Sam, worried by the thought. 'Like, you know, when I'm older.'

'I think the trick is to never stop believing,' said Sherlock.

They continued on along the road. They'd only walked a short distance when Sam turned his head at the sound of frantic barking. Coming along the road behind them was a little bronze Skye Terrier with a bright golden nose.

'Bobby!' cried Sam.

'Oh my giddy aunt,' said Sherlock.

And the three of them walked on together.

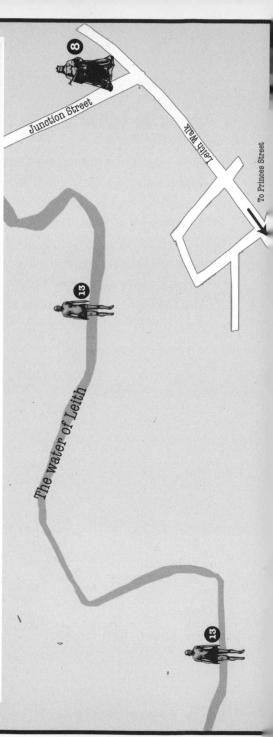

1. Royal Scot's Greys Memorial
West Princes St

2. David Livingstone
East Princes St. Gardens

3. Sir Walter Scott
East Princes St. Gardens

4. King Charles II
Behind Parliament Sq.

5. Dreaming Spires
Omni Centre, Picardy Roundabout

6. Sherlock Holmes
Picardy Place

7. Greyfriars Bobby
George IV Bridge

8. Queen Victoria
Foot of Leith Walk

9. Prince Albert
Charlotte Square Gardens

10. Woman and Child
Lothian Road

11. William Wallace
Edinburgh Castle Gatehouse

12. James Clerk Maxwell
East end of George Street

13. The Gormleys
Various, along the Water of Leith

Junction Street

Leith Walk

To Princes Street

The water of Leith

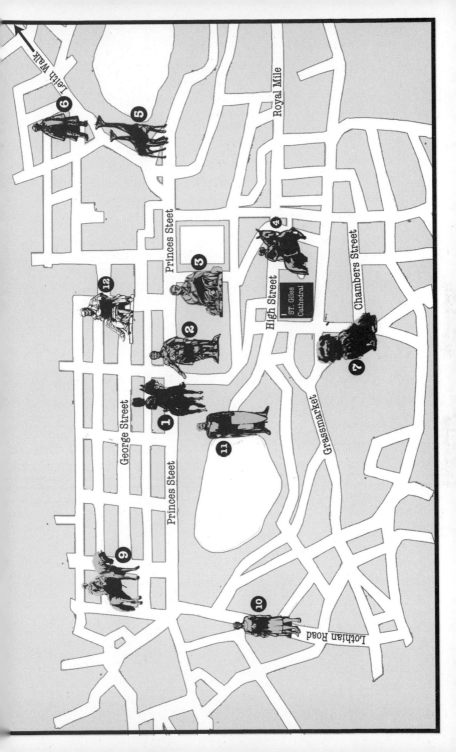

More Philip Caveney Titles

by Fledgling Press

The Crow Boy Trilogy

Crow Boy

Seventeen Coffins

One for Sorrow

Read on for the first chapter of Crow Boy

One

Tom stood in the pouring rain with the other kids from his class and waited for the coach. It was April, but felt cold enough for December. His classmates, boys and girls alike, were bundled up in heavy coats and parkas; they'd known what to expect. Tom had only his maroon blazer, which was already wet through.

It was hard not to feel sorry for himself. He hated Edinburgh, he hated his new school and he hated his classmates. And, what was worse, they hated him.

Oh, he could see that under different circumstances, Edinburgh would be a really cool place to visit. But he was here against his will. Only a week ago, he'd been in Manchester, hanging out with his friends, going to the movies, playing computer games, all the usual stuff. Any excuse not to spend too much time at home. He'd known for a long time that something was wrong between his parents; he'd suffered their long, deep silences, the sudden arguments that blew up out of nowhere but he'd chosen to stay out of it, telling himself that they were adults; they were supposed to know what they were doing . . .

And then, one Friday, he strolled out of school, looking forward to the weekend, and his Mum was waiting for him, sitting in the passenger seat of a car he'd never seen before, a sleek black Alfa Romeo.

There was this guy at the wheel of the car, a thickset man with a scrubby beard and receding hair. Mum wound down the window and said, 'Hi, Tom, get in.'

So he climbed into the back seat, bewildered, and Mum gestured at the driver and said, 'This is Hamish,' like it was supposed to mean something. Then Hamish gunned the engine and they set off.

'Where we going?' Tom asked apprehensively.

'Scotland,' she said, breezily, like she'd just announced they were nipping down the shops. 'Edinburgh. We're going to have a bit of a holiday.'

'For the weekend, you mean?'

'Umm . . . maybe a bit longer.'

'But . . . it's the middle of term,' he reminded her.

'Don't worry about that. I think you're entitled to a few days off every now and then.'

But of course, it was more than that. On the long . . . the very long journey North, Mum gradually revealed more and more about what was going on. She and Dad hadn't been getting on for a long time now. They'd drifted apart. She'd met Hamish through work, three months back. He was a rep, a kind of travelling salesman for a company that made shower fittings. He was based in Edinburgh, a really cool city. She kept saying that last bit as though trying to convince Tom that what they were doing was a good idea. Or maybe she was just trying to convince herself.

Anyway, she went on, she and Hamish were just made for each other; they were on the same wavelength.

They had so many interests in common. Hamish liked dancing and Dad would never do anything like that, he'd always been so reserved. Mum and Hamish liked the same music, the same films, the same holiday destinations . . .

Tom sat in the back seat and felt an awful sinking feeling deep inside, as he realised what she was really telling him. They were leaving Dad. They were leaving Manchester. He knew that he should be shouting about this, telling them to stop the car and let him out, but he was in shock and he could only sit there and listen while his mother prattled on. Hamish had this really fabulous house in a 'sought-after' part of Edinburgh, she told him. He was a widower, his wife had died a couple of years ago and, when he'd met Mum, something had just clicked between them; something incredible, something magical.

'It was like, I don't know, fate or something?' said Mum. She sounded like some love-struck teenager, not like a married woman of thirty-eight. 'We just looked at each other across the room and it was like it was all meant to be, you know what I mean? I thought to myself, Mary, you only get the one chance at happiness and you need to do something about this now, or spend the rest of your life regretting it.'

Through all this, Hamish just sat at the wheel, staring at the road ahead, his eyes narrowed down to slits against the sunlight, an unpleasant smirk on his potato-like face. Occasionally, he lifted one hand from the steering wheel and placed it on Mum's hand and Tom noticed a crude tattoo on his bare arm which read *Scotland Forever*. He didn't look anything like Dad, Tom thought. He looked like an oik, a loser. But Mum just kept on about how wonderful he was, how good he was with kids (he'd raised two of his own; they were grown now, and both of them had responsible jobs), he was a football fan and he'd run a couple of marathons for charity.

Tom finally pulled himself together enough to throw in a couple of objections. What about Mum's job at the catalogue company? What about school?

'Oh, I can walk into another job any time. You know I've always hated working for the catalogue, and as for school, there's a really good comprehensive just a stone's throw from Hamish's house in Fairmilehead, both of his kids went there, we can get you in, no problem! Edinburgh's a fantastic place, it has a castle, seaside, a mountain . . . oh, and the festival every summer! All that stand-up comedy, you'll love that! And listen, you can tell this was meant to be because the school has the same maroon blazers you wear at St Thomas's; all I'll need to do is sew on a new badge!'

'What about my friends?' he pleaded, but she hadn't faltered.

'You'll soon make new ones,' she told him. 'An easy-going lad like you, it'll only take you a few days . . .'

But of course the reality had been so different. From the moment he'd walked into his first class and Mr

McKenzie, his form teacher, had introduced him as 'the new arrival,' he'd been a marked man. The other kids spent all their time whispering about him, the 'The Manky,' a blow-in, laughing every time he opened his mouth and spoke in his flat Mancunian accent, imitating him when he was almost, but not quite, out of earshot. He felt like telling them that he hadn't asked to be here, that he hadn't had any say in the matter, but what difference would that have made? He wasn't welcome, simple as that.

And neither did he feel welcome at home. Hamish's 'cool' house had turned out to be a large semi on an anonymous side street of Fairmilehead. It had probably been nice enough once but, after three years of Hamish living there alone, it was looking decidedly scruffy. Whenever Tom was there with Mum and Hamish, he felt as though he was in the way, that they wanted to be alone, so he spent most of his time in his bedroom, the one that had previously belonged to Hamish's eldest son. With its Hibernian F.C. wallpaper and yellowing posters of grinning footballers, it looked as though nobody had been in there for years.

'We'll soon get this decorated more to your taste,' Hamish assured him when he and Mum had first taken him to look at the room. And then he reached out a big hand and tousled Tom's hair. 'I expect you're a United fan, eh?'

Tom had no interest in football whatsoever, and he

certainly didn't like Hamish touching him, but he said nothing, just shrugged his shoulders.

'We'll get you a computer,' Mum had added and Hamish had given her an odd look, a kind of a pursed-lip scowl, as if to say 'we'll have to see about that.' When they'd left him to 'make himself at home,' Tom had lain down on the bed and curled himself up into a foetal position, feeling that he wanted to cry, but not allowing himself the comfort of it.

And now, here he was, three weeks later, and he was going on a school trip to something or somewhere called Mary King's Close. When he'd brought the letter home from school, Mum had been keen for Tom to go but Hamish had said that he'd been to it, it was a con, just a trudge along some dirty old streets and not worth the money the school was asking. Mum still hadn't managed to 'walk into' that new job she'd mentioned and Hamish seemed to be watching the pennies. Mum had argued that Tom needed to get out a bit, it would help him make friends, and Hamish said that visiting some old ruin wasn't going to help the kid do that, he needed to stand up for himself a bit more. Right then and there, the couple who were 'so right for each other' had proceeded to have their first row. Tom thought about telling them that he didn't care whether he went or not, but they seemed to have forgotten he was there so he slunk off to his room and left them to it.

Mum must have prevailed though, because the money had been paid and now here was the coach, lurching out of the pouring rain like a giant caterpillar. It came to a halt with a loud hiss of air brakes. Then everyone was piling aboard, pushing and shoving to be first. Tom waited till everyone else was on and then he climbed the steps and trudged along the aisle until he found a seat to himself, as far away as possible from the most vocal of his tormentors, a kid called Stuart Gillies; a big overweight thug of a lad with spiky blonde hair, who took great delight in referring to Tom as 'The Manky.' Gillies was big enough and hard enough to have a small following of admirers who would do just about anything to be in his gang. If slagging off Tom was the price of admission, they were more than willing to join in.

As Tom slid into his seat, he heard Gillies' voice announcing that, 'The Manky looks like a drowned rat this morning.' This caused some laughter and then another voice, a girl called Jenny, added that it was a pity the Manky's Ma couldn't afford to buy him a coat. 'Oh, they don't wear coats in Manchester,' Gillies assured her. 'Too cool for that.' He adopted a poor Mancunian accent. 'They all think they're Liam bleedin' Gallagher!'

Tom tried to ignore him and stared fixedly out of the window at the rain-lashed street. A tramp in a frayed overcoat was pushing a supermarket trolley piled with his tattered belongings along the pavement, a few wet strands of grey hair plastered to his head. Somehow, he was managing to smoke a roll up, the thin stream of smoke rising between the daggers of rain. Some of the kids at the back of the coach started banging on the window and shouting to him. He looked up and flicked a casual V in their direction with two nicotine-stained fingers.

Mr McKenzie pulled his gangling figure aboard and stood at the front of the coach, doing a quick headcount. He was wearing a camel-coloured duffel coat which somehow made him look like an extra from a movie about World War Two. Then he made an announcement.

'I'd just like to remind everyone that you're representing your school today and we'd like you to act with the necessary decorum.'

This was met with a barrage of groans, laughs and jeers, but he soldiered gamely on.

'Also, don't forget that this is an educational trip, not a holiday. You will each be asked to submit an essay about the Plague of 1645, so I would advise you all to listen attentively to everything you hear today.'

Another long groan. Mr McKenzie gestured to the driver and took a seat at the front of the coach. It pulled away with another hiss of hydraulics and started along the street. Rain streaked diagonally across the window. Tom tried to concentrate his attention on the view but couldn't quite manage to shut out the voices coming from the back of the coach.

'I heard the Manky's mother did a runner on her old man,' said a voice.

'Aye,' agreed Gillies. 'Left him high and dry in Mankyland. Fancied a bit of local talent instead.'

'She's shacked up with Hamish McPherson,' said Jenny. 'I heard my Ma telling her friend.'

'Hamish McPherson. Jesus! She likes to live dangerously. Hamish McPherson with the . . .' The voice lowered to a whisper towards the end of the sentence so Tom couldn't hear what was said, but the derisive laughter at the end suggested that it had been fairly crude.

'Keep it down at the back!' shouted Mr McKenzie and the laughter faded. 'Stuart, don't let me have to tell you again.'

Tom sighed. He wondered what his friends were doing now. In Manchester, he'd have been joining in with the laughter and some other kid would have been the butt of the joke, some spod that everybody made fun of. Here, he was the outsider and it wasn't a nice place to be.

He reached into his pocket and took out his mobile, keeping it well out of sight because school rules didn't allow pupils to have them. It was Pay As You Go, and he was currently out of credit. Mum, sensing perhaps that he would be phoning his dad, had refused point blank to fund the habit, and he'd had to resort to using his dinner money but that only went so far.

The phone had been his lifeline over the past few weeks: he'd texted all his mates back in Manchester, telling them of his woes and, at first, they'd replied to him, expressing their concerns and making vague plans to come up there and rescue him. But, as time went on, they texted less often and now seemed to have given up on him completely. But he'd been texting his dad too and Dad had been texting him back, several times a day and had even phoned him a couple of times.

Dad claimed to have had no inkling about Mum's affair; the first he had known of it was when he got back from work and found the house empty and a letter on the mantelpiece. He had now put the matter in the hands of his solicitors (whatever that meant) and they were trying to find a way that Dad and Tom could be allowed to spend some time together – but the distances involved meant it could take quite a while to do that. In the meantime, Tom was to 'keep his chin up' and work hard at his new school, try to fit in as best he could. The last text Tom had received was an odd one and made him think that his Dad must have been drinking when he wrote it.

Tom. Please remember I will always love you. Dad.

As far as Tom could remember, it was the first time his dad had ever said those words to him.

He sighed and, determined to take his mind off his troubles, he loaded up *Timeslyp* on his phone, a game he'd been playing a lot lately. In it, the hero, John Kane, a lean, craggy man dressed in a wide-brimmed hat and a long leather coat, spent all his time running along endless corridors, dodging attacks from cloaked and masked assassins. They came out of the most unexpected places, leaping through paintings on the wall, oozing up from the bare floorboards beneath Kane's feet, dropping through the ceiling onto his back. He escaped them by performing a series of athletic leaps and somersaults to avoid the razor-sharp sickles they carried. Every so often, Kane would reach a doorway, a portal into another level and, whenever he burst through one of them, he would find himself in an alternate reality, where everything was slightly different and where the rules learned on the previous level no longer applied. It was weirdly addictive. Tom was currently on level six but couldn't quite seem to reach the next doorway. Every time he got close to it, he would be felled by a couple of assassins who jumped out of the shadows, hell-bent on his destruction.

He was so engrossed in the game that it was a complete surprise when the coach, with a great hissing of air brakes, pulled to a halt on the High Street and Mr McKenzie announced that it was time to get off. Tom abandoned the game, noting as he did so that the phone's battery was half gone.

'Great,' he muttered. He shoved the phone into his damp blazer pocket and waited for the other kids to leave the coach before tagging reluctantly along behind them.